OUTLAW ROUNDUP

Hidden in the night, Slade and his men watched the smugglers' boat being poled across the Rio Grande. As the craft touched the bank, the contraband buyers swarmed to meet it — and five horsemen pounded into sight, shooting as they came! Screams and curses echoed the reports as the smugglers and their customers fell to the bullets from the dark. Slade sent his horse pounding down the slope — his own guns blazing — toward a showdown with the man he had hunted for so long . . .

BRADFORD SCOTT

◆

OUTLAW ROUNDUP

Complete and Unabridged

LINFORD
Leicester

First published in the
United States of America

First Linford Edition
published March 1994

British Library CIP Data

Scott, Bradford
    Outlaw roundup.—Large print ed.—
Linford western library
I. Title II. Series
823.914 [F]

ISBN 0–7089–7500–3

Published by
F. A. Thorpe (Publishing) Ltd.
Anstey, Leicestershire

Set by Words & Graphics Ltd.
Anstey, Leicestershire
Printed and bound in Great Britain by
T. J. Press (Padstow) Ltd., Padstow, Cornwall

This book is printed on acid-free paper

1

IN 1877, the Man of Destiny entered Brownsville, Texas, unheralded and unsung, and established himself in a house on Thirteenth Street.

Brownsville, with that establishment as the hub, became a hotbed of plots and counterplots, and in that house were planned the initial moves of a campaign that opened with the capture of the Mexican town of Matamoros across the Rio Grande from Brownsville and swept onward in the successful revolution that made the Man of Destiny, Porfirio Diaz, dictator of Mexico.

The citizens of Brownsville watched with dubious interest the progress of that revolution. The interest became more dubious and the fiery-eyed reformer and champion of the masses changed to a querulous old codger with outlandish notions that he put into effect to the detriment of both Mexico and Texas.

As a whole, the people of the two towns got along very well together, passing back and forth across the Gateway Bridge at the foot of Fourteenth Street SE., sharing fiestas, intermarrying, trading.

Although not much older than Brownsville, Matamoros had been battered and battle-scarred into a semblance of antiquity. It had been burned twice and pillaged more than once. During abortive uprisings, which were not infrequent, Brownsville absorbed both refugees and bullets. These, however, were taken in stride as necessary irritations like taxes and the perennial spoutings of politicians.

For the next quarter of a century or so after the departure of Diaz on his march of conquest, Brownsville maintained a fairly peaceful state of existence. Outlaws rode the neighboring brush country. Bands of cattle thieves were well organized and plied their questionable trade expertly. Pirates made river traffic lively, and riding the trails, especially at night, was hazardous. Death from various violent causes maintained a fairly stable rate. Brownsville, although it now dignified itself as a city, was still a wild frontier border town with all the trimmin's.

Ranger Walt Slade, named by the *peóns* of the Rio Grande river villages *El Halcón* — The Hawk — was thinking of all this as he rode the last leg of the thirty-mile jaunt from Isabel — his destination, Brownsville on the Rio Grande.

"Yes, it's Brownsville again," Captain Jim McNelty, the famed commander of the Border Battalion of the Texas Rangers, had growled to his lieutenant and undercover ace man. "That blankety-blank town is the worst on the river. Oh, the same old story — robberies, murders, cow stealin', steamboats robbed, one sank. Same old story, but always with a new wrinkle. Now there's no doubt another phony

3

liberator risin' up south of the border and promisin' everybody the world with a fence around it if they do as he says. Seems to be a smart one, too, if there is one, judgin' from what Sheriff Tom Calder wrote in his letter squawkin' for help.

"Okay, amble down there and straighten things out. Then sift sand back here; I'll have somethin' else for you to do. And tell Tom Calder I said to stir his stumps and try actin' like a sheriff for a change."

Slade chuckled to himself as he recalled Captain Jim's last remark and anticipated what Sheriff Calder, a decidedly able veteran of the border turmoil, would have to say when it was delivered to him.

"Well, Shadow," Slade observed to his magnificent black horse, "those lights ahead are Brownsville. We should make it to the pueblo in another twenty minutes or so. Where we'll have a chance to put on the nosebag, which we can both use about now."

Shadow, evidently understanding that oats were referred to, quickened his gait a bit. Slade tweaked his ear and was rewarded for his temerity by a snap of teeth as white and even as his own, that just grazed the leg of his overalls and would have done more than graze had Shadow really meant business.

Having mutually affronted each other, they jogged on with the cluster of lights, like fallen stars, growing larger and brighter. Soon they could hear the hum of the busy town, loudening as they drew near. It lacked little more than an hour to midnight, but Brownsville citizens had their share of owl blood and were not given to early retiring.

Slade entered Brownsville by way of Elizabeth Street, his first stop a stable kept by an elderly Mexican. Tapping on the door brought the owner, nursing a sawed-off six-gauge shotgun, the hour being late and strangers sometimes questionable. He and Slade were old *amigos* and they shook hands warmly, albeit the keeper's clasp was somewhat diffident, and he bowed low to *El Halcón*.

He had formerly been introduced to Shadow, a one-man horse who allowed no one to put a hand on him without his master's sanction, and he led the tall black to a stall and a helpin' of oats.

"Still got the big trough of cold water in back?" Slade asked.

"*Si, Capitán*, to the brimming full, and cold, for from the spring deep down it comes. Honored it will be to serve *El Halcón*, the good, the just, the compassionate, the friend of the lowly. Here, *Capitán*." He handed Slade a bar of soap and a large, rough towel.

A leisurely sluice in the icy waters of the trough, a brisk rubdown, and the ranger felt greatly refreshed and looked forward with pleasurable anticipation to something to eat.

He had barely started donning his clothes when suddenly the stable rocked and quivered to a booming explosion, not far off. The horses neighed with fright.

"*Cien mil diablos!*" yelled Agosto, the keeper.

Slade went on with his dressing at top speed. The horses were snorting, Agosto yammering incoherently. Now whistles were wailing in the harbor. From no great distance came yells and a crackle of gunfire. Slade seized his double cartridge belts and buckled them in place. Hands close to the black butts of the big Colts snugged in their carefully worked and oiled cutout holsters, he bounded to the door, flung it open. Even as he did so, half a dozen horsemen swerved into the alley on which the stable stood, shooting back over their shoulders. One sighted the ranger's tall form in the doorway, whipped his gun to the front and sent a slug into the doorpost scant inches from *El Halcón*'s head.

Walt Slade didn't like being shot at by perfect strangers; he signified his dissent in no uncertain terms. A howl

7

of pain, and another echoed the bellow of his Colts. He saw an arm swing limp, a second rider lunge forward, grabbing the horn for support.

Slade did not shoot to kill, for he wasn't sure just what it was all about. When he finally got the lowdown, he wished he had. As it was, back inside the door as the horsemen swept past, he contented himself with sending a couple of bullets whining close over their heads. He ducked instinctively as behind him sounded a roar. A blast of hot air fanned the back of his neck. Agosto had let go both barrels of his six-gauge as the riders swerved around the far corner.

"Hold it!" Slade told him. "You'll blow the town into the river with that old baseburner."

"Men come," said Agosto.

Men were appearing at the near mouth of the alley, poking cautious heads around the corner of the building. Apparently reassured by Slade's appearance, they streamed into the alley.

"Did you get 'em, cowboy?" one shouted. The others volleyed more questions that made little sense. Slade's great voice rolled in thunder to still the tumult.

"Quiet down," he ordered. "I can't make head or tail of what you're saying. What does this mean? Where was the explosion?"

"They blew up the stage station — it's on fire!" somebody howled. The hullabaloo began afresh.

In the distance sounded a clanging of bells, drawing nearer. Evidently the Brownsville fire company was answering the alarm set off by the boat whistles in the harbor.

"Here comes the sheriff!" a voice yelled.

Lean old Sheriff Tom Calder shouldered his way through the crowd. He halted, stared.

"Well, I'll be hanged!" he exploded. "Might have knowed it. The minute you hit town all hell busts loose. Never knew it to fail."

9

"Well, you sent for me, didn't you?" Slade countered.

"I sure did," Calder acknowledged. "How are you, Walt? Good to see you again." They shook hands heartily.

The crowd was streaming back to the burning station, where the fire fighters had evidently arrived and were unlimbering their equipment.

"Just what happened, Tom?" Slade asked. "Sounded like the sky had fallen in."

"Oh, best as I could judge from a quick look, the hellions blew open the station office safe and cleaned it, working mighty fast. Must have used a mite too much powder — blew the safe door clean across the room. Stray sparks must have set fire to the heavy window curtains. They set fire to the sashes, and the flames ran up the side of the building, which is tinder-dry — no rain for quite a while. Guess they cleaned the safe, all right, and high-tailed before anybody realized just what was going on. Came through

10

the alley, didn't they? How come you didn't do for a few?"

"I'd just finished bathing in the stable trough," Slade explained. "Heard the explosion, of course. Thought for a minute the stable was going to cave in. By the time I got some clothes on and made it to the door, the bunch was coming down the alley, shooting back over their shoulders. One threw a slug at me, missed; so I figure they should be discouraged. Nicked a couple, I think. Didn't shoot to kill because I didn't know just what it was all about. Otherwise, I'd have shifted my sights a trifle."

"A pity you didn't," growled the sheriff. "But I know how you feel. So darn many private rukuses cutting loose in this hell-town that a feller don't know where he stands; hates to horn in on something that's a strictly personal matter and none of his business."

2

"WELL, suppose we mosey over to the stage station and see what's what," Slade suggested. "Imagine the fire boys have got the blaze under control by now."

"Yep, I don't think it amounted to more than some scorched planks," Calder replied. "Let's go!"

Slade turned and patted old Agosto's shoulder. "*Gracias, amigo*," he said. "Guess you sort of put the finishing touches on the hellions."

"Would that I had been able to fire sooner," regretted the keeper. "*Capitán*, I had to dodge around."

"Glad you took time to," Slade chuckled. "A pity, though, that you didn't get the chance to throw down on the bunch. If you had, I'm of the opinion that old Doc, the coroner,

12

would have had something to hold an inquest on."

"That thing would have taken care of all six of the devils," said the sheriff, gazing somewhat askance at the monstrous twin muzzles of the six-gauge. "Let's go, 'fore it takes a notion to cut loose of itself." Slade laughed, and they left the alley.

"Nobody killed this time?" he asked.

"Guess not," answered Calder. "Understand the station manager had locked up and left just a little while before it happened. Reckon they watched him leave and slipped in right afterward."

"No doubt," Slade agreed.

When they reached the station, they found the blaze had been drenched down to steaming smoulders. Calder's two deputies were present and had kept everybody out except the firemen, who were stacking their equipment and preparing to depart.

"And keep 'em out till I give the word," the sheriff ordered as he and Slade entered the office.

The big old iron safe stood open, the heavy door blown clean across the room, an inner drawer smashed open and evidently looted of its money contents. On the floor near the safe lay a hand-drill, the steel bit still in the brace. Beside it were a tin container and a small funnel.

"A smart bunch, all right," Slade commented. "Must have worked like a machine, considering the short period they had in which to operate. Hang onto that drill; it's a good instrument, and we might be able to trace back to where it was sold and, possibly, who purchased it. Unlikely, but we mustn't pass up any chances. Yes, very clever hellions, and knew their business. Only their powder man miscalculated a little and used a trifle too much soup; a wonder he didn't blow the building down."

"Soup?" the sheriff questioned.

"Nitroglycerin," Slade explained. "Bored a hole in the door; that steel bit would cut into the iron of that old safe like it was cheese. Poured in the soup between the door casings and set it off with a short fuse and a percussion cap. Have one of the boys throw that container and the funnel in the river. There could be enough nitro clinging to the sides to injure somebody handling them carelessly."

At that moment the station manager came hurrying in, his face mirroring concern.

"Just heard about it," he announced. "That is that it happened here. Guess everybody this side of Laredo heard the explosion. Blast it! Why couldn't I have stuck around a little longer instead of leaving when I did?"

"You can consider yourself fortunate that you did leave," Slade told him grimly. "Otherwise you'd have quite likely gotten a knife in your back or a gun barrel bent over your skull. That bunch wouldn't have tolerated interruption."

The manager looked a bit dazed.

15

"You — you mean they would have killed me?"

"At least close to it," Slade replied.

"You're darn right they would have," interpolated the sheriff. "Remember what happened to that poor devil of a saloonkeeper they robbed; he never knew what hit him."

The manager shuddered. "But I've a notion that with Mr. Slade here with us again, the scoundrels won't find such easy pickings from now on," he said.

"You can say that a coupla times," grunted the sheriff. Slade deftly changed the subject.

"Did they get much?"

"Yes," said the manager. "I can't say as to the exact amount until I check the books, but it was plenty. Money from San Benito consigned to the bank. Had to do with a real estate deal, I understand. Got in too late to make the bank, so I stowed it in the safe, thinking it would be all right. Guess I was wrong. We are insured, of course, but I'm afraid it will skyrocket our rates."

Slade was silent a moment, then: "Don't you have a night watchman on duty?"

"Why, yes," replied the manager. "But tonight he sent word that he was sick and couldn't make it. I was unable to get a replacement on such short notice."

"Did you know the messenger who brought the word?" Slade asked.

The manager shook his head. "Can't say as I recall seeing him before," he answered.

Slade asked another question: "Do you know where the watchman lives?"

"Over on Monroe Street, where he has a little place of his own. A fine old fellow — been with us for years."

"Suppose we take a walk over there," Slade suggested.

"Why, of course, if you wish to," replied the manager. "Do you think — "

"I don't think anything, except his illness came mighty pat to fit in with

17

the robbers' plans," Slade interrupted. "Let's go."

Outside, Calder said to the deputies, "Come along, Gus. Webley, you stay here till we get back."

It was no great distance to the little cottage on Monroe Street where the watchman resided, and the manager set a fast pace. The house was dark when they reached it, and as they approached the door, Slade's keen ears caught a sound of thumping and a muffled muttering and grumbling.

"Not dead, at least," he remarked in relieved tones. He shoved open the door and struck a match. The tiny flicker showed a nearby bracket lamp and a moving form on the floor. He touched the match to the lamp wick, and a mellow glow filled the room.

The form on the floor proved to be an elderly man with blood dabbling his grizzled hair back of the right temple. His wrists and ankles were securely tied together, and a neckerchief bound over his mouth held a gag in place. He was thrashing about and mumbling back of the gag.

Kneeling beside him, Slade jerked the gag from his mouth and with a couple of slashes of his knife freed wrists and ankles.

The watchman, for of course it was he, let loose a flood of appalling profanity and struggled to a sitting position, with Slade's help.

"Take it easy," the Ranger admonished. "Take it easy, and tell us what happened." The soothing voice calmed the old fellow.

"Hardly know myself," he replied, while Slade examined the cut in his scalp. "Was fixin' my lunch when I heard somethin' and turned around. Saw two big hellions loomin' over me. That's about all I did see 'cept a shower of stars and comets. Guess they pistol whipped me and knocked me cold. Don't know how long it was till I got my senses back and found myself all trussed like a pig for a roastin'. Couldn't get myself loose;

could just wiggle and thump and try to talk. Say, I'm plumb glad to see you fellers. Was beginnin' to think I was a goner; wasn't breathin' too well through that handkerchief stuffed in my mouth."

Slade nodded and turned to the deputy. "Fetch the doctor," he directed. "Don't think the gentleman is badly hurt, but we'll take no chances.

"Think you can sit up if I help you to a chair?" he asked the watchman.

"Sure," the oldster replied. "Just lend me a hand." Another moment and he was sitting comfortably, Slade padding the wound with a clean handkerchief and securing the pad in place with the neckerchief that had served as a gag.

"Is the other room a kitchen?" he asked.

"That's right," said the watchman. "Plenty of good chuck layin' around if you hanker for a snack. Pot of coffee on the stove. Had oughta still be plenty warm; was a good bed of coals under it."

"Tom, see if it is hot; if it isn't, heat it up a bit," Slade told the sheriff. "Hot coffee is good for a person who has suffered shock."

Calder hurried to the kitchen and lit another lamp. "I'd say it's still plenty hot," he called. "I'll bring him a cup."

While the watchman was drinking his coffee, the doctor arrived. He shook hands with Slade. "Any indications of fracture?" he asked.

"None that I could ascertain," the Ranger replied.

"Then there ain't," said the doctor. "Those hands of yours miss nothing. I'll tie him up and put him to bed.

"Chances are you saved the old coot's life, getting here like you did," he added, after Calder had supplied details. "He'd very likely have choked to death on that gag before somebody showed up in the afternoon looking for him."

"It was Mr. Slade's idea," put in the manager.

"He's always got the right idea," grunted Doc, giving a final pat to the bandage he had applied over the padded wound.

"I'll stay with him for a while," said the manager. "Tom, tell your deputy to put out the lights and shut the door, and to heck with the station; nothing worth stealing in there now."

"Okay, Alf," answered the sheriff. "See you tomorrow."

"And I don't think you need fear an encore tonight," Slade said smilingly. "Let's go, Tom. I'll pick up my pouches at the stable and register for a room at the hotel, and then the Blue Bell and something to eat before I topple over from hunger. Be seeing you, everybody."

It was well past midnight when they belatedly reached the big Blue Bell saloon and restaurants, but there was still plenty of business. Lanky, saturnine Fats Boyer, the owner, welcomed Slade with enthusiasm and steered them to a table.

"The one you always liked, Mr. Slade," he said. "It'll be held open for you from now on. Don't bother to order; I'll tell the cook who's here, and he'll rustle something special for *El Halcón*. Waiter! Drinks, and keep 'em coming. Everything on the house."

Grinning broadly, he hurried to the kitchen. The old Mexican cook stuck his head out the door and waved a greeting, which Slade returned.

"I was thinking of what Doc said," the sheriff remarked thoughtfully. "I've a notion you did save that old watchman's life by getting to him pronto."

"It is possible," Slade conceded. "His face was already beginning to purple when we got there. The neckerchief was tight over his nose as well as his mouth. While he lay unconscious, the lack of oxygen was not affecting him so much, but when he began to move around and his heart-beat accelerated, it was different."

The sheriff nodded his understanding. "What I can't figure," he said, "is why the sidewinders didn't kill somebody, the way they were sprayin' lead in every direction as they rode away from the station."

"I would say," Slade replied, "that some member of the bunch, presumably the leader, is to an extent a psychologist. Bullets whistling over peoples' heads make them duck and dodge, not knowing for sure what it's all about; whereas a killing displaces fear with anger and an urge to retaliate. Remember, I did not shoot to kill because I was not sure just what it was all about."

"All of which, I guess, means the horned toads figured in advance a way to get in the clear," Calder sighed.

"Exactly," Slade agreed. "Incidentally, I don't think the window drapes were ignited by a stray spark, as everybody presumes. I believe the fire was deliberately set to further distract attention. Oh, it's a smart bunch, all right, and if they are responsible for all the things I understand have been happening — you can tell me more about it later — it looks like we have our work cut out for us."

"Guess you're right again," growled the sheriff, eyeing his empty glass with disapproval and hammering for a refill. "Let us drink!"

3

THEIR meal arrived, and there followed a period of busy silence as they addressed themselves to the food with appetite. Finally Slade rolled a cigarette and ordered a final cup of steaming coffee. Calder loaded his old black pipe.

"What you been up to since you were here last?" he asked. "Hardly hoped to see you so soon again."

"Seems I'm always starting from the west and working east," Slade replied. "I was at El Paso, then Sanderson, then Laredo, and now here again."

"And the worst of the lot," snorted the sheriff.

"This section has much to attract outlaws," Slade pointed out. "Especially the smart brand we are getting nowadays, carefully planning their raids with scrupulous attention to details, not making many slips. Shrewd, daring, resourceful. All too often, utterly ruthless. Sometimes afflicted by the blood lust, as was the case with Webster Mahanes when I was here last."

"And you gave him his comeuppance," Calder observed. "Wonder why the hellions left the old watchman alive and just tied up instead of knifing him to death?"

"You can rest assured it was not through kindness of heart," Slade answered. "They must have had a reason for doing so, and I'd certainly like to know what it was. I hope to have a talk with him later; he might be able to supply some additional information; his mind was still rather foggy tonight, so I didn't question him more. And you have no idea as to the identity of the bunch?"

"Not a notion," Calder replied. "Fact is, I've sorta been feeling that there's more than one bunch raising heck in the section."

"That is possible," Slade admitted,

"although I rather lean to the belief that it is just one well-organized and competent outfit. How about the liberator talk Captain Jim mentioned?"

"Oh, there's always that sort of talk going around," said the sheriff. "Haven't heard anything definite so far. If there is one, he's out of the ordinary, I'd say."

"And it would seem that the robberies, wideloopings and pirating fall into a pattern," Slade commented. "Which, I think, substantiates my notion that there is but one bunch. Well, this afternoon I'll amble across the bridge to Matamoros for a little gabfest with Amado Menendez, the owner of the La Luz cantina. Amado always has a pretty good notion of what's going on and has been a big help in the past. Maybe he will know something that may prove of value."

"Dolores Malone is still working there," the sheriff remarked insinuatingly.

"I'll be glad to see her again, too," Slade replied smilingly. "Now

I'm heading back to the kitchen to thank the cook and have a word with his boys."

Glances followed Slade's progress to the kitchen, for he was a man to attract attention in any gathering. He was very tall, more than six feet. The breadth of his shoulders and the depth of his chest matched his splendid height, and his movements were rhythmic perfection.

His face was as arresting as his form. A rather wide mouth, grin-quirked at the corners, relieved somewhat the tinge of fierceness evinced by the prominent hawk nose above and the powerful jaw and chin beneath. His hair, surmounting a broad forehead, was thick and crisp, and as black as his horse Shadow's midnight coat. The sternly handsome countenance was dominated by long, blacklashed eyes of very pale gray — cold, reckless eyes that nevertheless seemed always to have gay little devils of laughter dancing in their clear depths, devils that, did occasion warrant, would leap to the front and be anything but laughing. Then the eyes became 'the terrible eyes of *El Halcón*' that had more than once been known to cause armed men to back down without making a hostile move.

Slade wore, with distinction and grace, the homely, efficient garb of the rangeland — Levis, the bibless overalls favored by cowhands, soft blue shirt with vivid neckerchief looped at his sinewy throat, well scuffed halfboots of softly tanned leather, and the broad-brimmed 'J.B.,' the rainshed of the plains, as the cowboys called a hat.

Around his lean waist were double cartridge belts, from the holsters of which protruded the plain black butts of heavy guns. And from the butts of those big Colts his slender, muscular hands seemed never far away.

Such was Walt Slade, Texas Ranger, Captain Jim McNelty's lieutenant and undercover ace-man, and — the highest compliment the rangeland can pay — 'a man to ride the river with!'

In the kitchen Slade thanked the

cook and his helpers for the excellence of the repast, complimented them on their culinary ability and left them beaming.

"Always does he remember the lowly," the old cook murmured. "Truly of *El Dios* chosen is he!"

Returning to the sheriff, Slade announced, "And now I'm going to bed. Been a long and busy day. See you after a session of ear pounding."

"The same for me," said Calder. "Be seeing you."

* ★ *

Around noon Slade awakened, feeling much rested and ready for anything. He bathed and shaved, donned a clean shirt and overalls and headed for the Blue Bell and breakfast, where he found Calder awaiting him, fortified with a glass of redeye.

They enjoyed a hearty meal, and then Slade suggested, "Suppose we pay the stage station watchman a visit? I want to have a few words with him."

"Okay with me," said the sheriff, and they set out.

They found the watchman up and about and feeling quite chipper. "As I said last night, I didn't get much of a look at the devils, but I did notice that one of 'em had a big jagged scar down the side of his face, and the other had a very broad and flat nose," he replied to Slade's question.

"So that's the sorta looking hellions we want to keep our eyes out for," growled Calder.

"Individuals of such an appearance are definitely *not* what we wish to keep a lookout for," Slade differed.

"Now what the devil do you mean by that?" demanded the sheriff.

"A clumsy but efficient disguise," Slade replied. "Grease paint, properly applied, can simulate a scar, and quills thrust up the nostrils will broaden and flatten a nose. They desired that the watchman should get a glimpse of them that way."

"Is there anything you don't see!" groaned the sheriff.

"Plenty," Slade answered. "But this is just too obvious. Gentlemen not wishing to be recognized don't walk in with their hats on the backs of their heads, their faces exposed. They either wear masks or have their hatbrims pulled low, their neckerchiefs up high. That pair desired that the watchman get a look at them and report them as he saw them, leaving the authorities chasing their tails around in circles looking for scar-faced and pug-nosed gents who don't exist. That's why, the chances are, they didn't kill him instead of just knocking him out."

"By gosh! It sounds plumb reasonable to me," said the watchman.

"Oh, he never misses a bet," Calder concurred wearily. "Makes the rest of us look like squirrel fodder."

The watchman seemed to think this remark very funny, although the sheriff had no intention of being humorous.

Saying goodbye to the watchman,

who said he expected to be on the job at night, they headed for the office, pausing at the stage station, where repairs were under way.

"And I'm getting a new safe, a steel one the hellions won't find so easy to drill holes in," the manager told them.

"The sensible thing to do," Slade replied. "That old box was perfectly useless where such an outfit was concerned. Be seeing you."

As they made their way to the office, Calder remarked, "I had Webley take that hand drill and make the rounds of the hardware stores and tool shops with it."

"A good idea," Slade agreed. "Very likely nothing will come of it, but there is a chance somebody might recall selling it and to whom. We don't want to pass up any bets. In the past, such a trifle has been productive of results."

"The way I felt about it," said Calder. "Well, here we are. Hope Gus has some coffee hot. I can stand a swig spiked with the bottle in the desk drawer."

Gus did have coffee simmering on the stove in the back room. Calder hauled out his bottle and did a chore of spiking. Slade took his straight.

"And now what?" Calder asked, when the cups were empty.

"Now I'm going to mosey across the bridge and have a talk with Amado Menendez," Slade replied.

"Okay, I'll be there for dinner," the sheriff replied. "Got a hankerin' for the sorta chuck the cook will dish up when you're around."

Slade wandered about town for a while, then made his way to the Gateway Bridge. The crown of the bridge was quite high — higher than necessary had been *El Halcón*'s opinion when he first viewed it with the eye of a trained engineer. In consequence, the approaches, north and south, were quite steep.

He walked slowly, enjoying the

beauty of the late afternoon. He reached the level expanse of the crowd, and a short distance from the dip of the south approach he paused, leaned on the rail and gazed at the brown and hurrying flood of the Rio Grande. He was thus occupied when he heard a beat of hoofs coming up from the north shore.

Another moment and three horsemen bulged into view, jogging along at a fair pace. They paid him no mind as they swept past, faces averted, talking among themselves. Slade idly watched them cover the few yards to the downward dip.

At the lip of the slant they whirled in their saddles.

But *El Halcón* was down and under the overhang of the rail a split second before the guns blazed. Bullets whined over him. One struck the floor of the bridge and knocked splinters in his face. He whipped out both Colts and let drive, saw one rider reel in the saddle even as they vanished from sight down the approach.

Scrambling erect, Slade bounded forward, guns ready, but held his fire. There were people moving about at the foot of the approach, and he didn't care to take the chance of winging one. They scattered wildly as the horsemen raced past them, going like the wind, and swerved west toward the Camino Real, the old post road from *presidio* to *presidio* in the days of the Spanish king, now little travelled.

With swift ease, Slade reloaded and holstered his guns. Then he strolled casually down the approach, at the foot of which profanity in several languages was turning the air blue.

"*Loco ladrónes*! They the hole shoot in the sky!" somebody bawled in broken English. "See you them, *Capitán*?"

"They had passed me when they began shooting," Slade answered, refraining to mention what they had been shooting *at*.

Skirting the still irate citizens of Matamoros, nodding and smiling to familiar faces, Slade paused to gaze west toward the *Camino Real*, presumably the route followed by the outlaws.

It had been a very neat try, and with the average person it might well have succeeded. Evidently the outlaws had spotted him walking about in Brownsville, had watched him ascend the bridge approach and decided it was a chance to get rid of a threat to their security.

Because of the ruckus in the alley by the stable, in the course of which he had undoubtedly nicked a couple of the bunch? It was possible, but Slade was more inclined to believe he had been recognized by the outlaws as *El Halcón* with a reputation in some quarters for horning in on the good things others had started, a pest that must be eradicated as quickly as possible. Yes, that was very likely it. Looked like his *El Halcón* reputation might pay off again. Appeared it was bringing the outlaws to him. From his way of viewing the situation this was all to the good, for he had no idea where to look for them. He gave little thought to the fact that such a contingency laid him open to grave personal danger.

Due to his habit of working alone and undercover whenever possible, often not revealing his Ranger connections, Walt Slade had built up a peculiar dual reputation. Those who knew the truth declared vigorously that he was not only the most fearless, but also the ablest of the Rangers; while others, who knew him only as *El Halcón* with killings to his credit, insisted that he was himself just an owlhoot too smart to get caught, so far.

However, others of this group were his stanch defenders, maintaining that he always worked on the side of law and order, often with peace officers of impeccable repute, and that anybody he killed had a killing coming.

The deception worried Captain McNelty, who was always afraid his lieutenant might meet with harm at the hands of some mistaken and overzealous marshal or deputy, or would be shot in the back by a professional gunslinger out to bolster his reputation by downing the fastest and most accurate gunhand in the whole Southwest.

But Slade would point out that as *El Halcón* he was able to garner information from sources closed to a known Ranger and that outlaws, thinking him just one of their own brand, sometimes grew careless, much to their disadvantage.

So Captain Jim would grumble but not specifically forbid the deception, and Slade would go his carefree way as *El Halcón*, not bothering at all about possible consequences, treasuring most what was said by the *peóns* and other humble persons: '*El Halcón*! The just, the good, the honorable, the friend of the lowly! May *El Dios* ever guard him and keep him from harm!'

4

THREADING his way through the Plaza de Hidalgos, around which life centered in Matamoros, and the City Market, Slade approached La Luz, Amado Menendez' commodious, tastefully appointed and softly lighted *cantina*.

Amado was at the far end of the bar when he entered, talking to a girl in the short, spangled skirt and low-cut bodice of the dance floor. She was a rather small girl, but her proportions certainly left nothing to be desired, especially from the masculine viewpoint. She had curly, glossy black hair, lots of it, a creamily tanned complexion with a few freckles powdering the bridge of her little straight nose, sweetly formed, very red lips, and very large, deeply blue eyes.

Big, jovial Amado instantly spotted

Slade as he pushed through the swinging doors, but his rubicund features moved not a muscle; only one eyelid drooped the merest trifle. He began speaking animatedly to the girl, whose back was to the door.

Slade drifted silently across the room, passing the few patrons present at this early hour. Miss Dolores Malone's first intimation of his presence was a resounding smack that caused her to jump a foot and let out a screech. She whirled around, her blue eyes blazing. But the wrathful scolding at such effrontery changed to a little gurgling cry of delight as she fairly flung herself in his arms.

"Darling!" she cried. "Is it really you? Or do I dream?"

"Didn't it feel like me?" he countered, holding her close.

"It certainly did," she giggled, giving the afflicted part, which still tingled, a surreptitious rub. "Oh, I'm so glad to see you and so wonderfully surprised that you returned to Dolores so soon. Or is it just a case of any old port in a storm, after all the others turned you down?"

"What others!" he replied with innocent indignation that caused her to giggle again.

"Never mind, You're here, and that's all I care about. Uncle Amado, why didn't you warn me he was coming up behind me? I won't be able to — to do anything comfortably but dance for a week!"

"There is work in the back room," Amado observed pointedly.

"Okay, I'll suffer," she replied. "Be seeing you, Walt, as soon as I escape from the clutches of the old slave driver." She whisked into the back room, closing the door behind her. Amado chuckled delightedly as he shook hands with Slade.

"Happy she now is," he said. "But come. The golden wine to this day we drink."

He led the way to a table where a

waiter was placing crystal goblets and a tawny bottle.

"Shooting we heard, at the distance," Amado remarked as he quaffed his wine. "To it we paid no mind, not knowing that *Capitán* was here. Does of it *Capitán* know?"

In answer, Slade detailed the incident on the bridge. Amado shook his big head sagely.

"Of the brain of the terrapin they are, else they would not have it tried," he commented. "So *El Halcón* they seek?"

"Looks a little that way," Slade conceded. "What about the liberator angle this time?"

"If there is one, shrewd he is," replied Amado. "None of the big talk is heard."

"I see," Slade said thoughtfully. "Which means, if there is one operating, he'll be harder to run down. Will pose more of a problem."

"Si, the sidewinder, who does not rattle, is the dangerous more," agreed

Amado, adding, "but *Capitán* will not fail."

Dolores bounced out of the back room and plopped into a chair, apparently not handicapped by her recent 'injury.' She passed Amado a paper.

"Some suggestions of which I thought you would approve," she said.

Amado took the paper and persued it gravely, nodding his agreement. Slade stifled a grin. It was an open secret that Dolores was the real manager of La Luz, whether Amado was present or not. And it was her shrewd business sense that was largely responsible for the *cantina*'s outstanding success.

Her father had been a handsome Irish soldier of fortune who had never amassed much of this world's goods. He had married Amado's older sister, who, like her niece, had inherited the famed beauty of the Menendez women. Dolores had inherited good looks from both parents. How she had come by her business acumen, nobody knew for sure — certainly not from either father or mother. When her father died, less than a year after his wife passed on, Amado would have gladly supported her, but Dolores felt that a Texas girl who could support herself should do so and went to work dancing in the *cantina*, gradually rising to her present position. She loved to dance and spent much time on the floor.

"Ha!" exclaimed Amado. "Another *amigo* approaches. Come, Estevan, and partake."

The newcomer was a tall young Yaquí-Mexican with a dark, savage face. His facial characteristics were those of one of the indomitable mountain *Indios*, but his superior height denoted much Spanish blood. He was the chief of Amado's 'young men' who helped him keep order in the *cantina*. He and Slade had shared stirring adventures in the past. He seemed to glide rather than walk as he made his way to the table to shake hands, diffidently, and bow low to *El Halcón*.

He sat down and accepted a glass of wine, regarding Slade with affection and respect.

"Nice to see you again, Estevan," Slade said.

"And most nice to you again see, *Capitán*," the other returned. In his eyes rose a hopeful look.

"And *Capitán* is business on?" he asked.

Slade chuckled. Estevan was never really happy unless he was embroiled in a contest of wits and knives, preferably knives.

"Wouldn't be surprised; in fact it looks sort of that way," the Ranger replied.

"Good!" Estevan exclaimed. "Ha! I and my *amigos* will listen and watch. Soon perhaps we will learn something of interest to *Capitán*."

"And that I don't doubt in the least," *El Halcón* said, and meant it. Very little went on along the river that Estevan and his *amigos* did not learn about.

Amado launched into a repeat of what Slade had said about the encounter on the bridge, embellishing the account with some observations of his own decidedly laudable to *El Halcón*.

"Makes it sound like I decimated an army," Slade protested. "Really, there wasn't much to it — just a try that didn't succeed. And I think one of the wind spiders has something by which to remember me."

"Hope I that he now is past remembering," said Estevan, his voice like steel grinding on jagged ice. He finished his glass, bowed again to *El Halcón*, and glided out to 'listen and watch.'

Sheriff Calder arrived, called for a surrounding, Slade electing to join him.

"Hellions ain't wasting any time, eh?" he growled when told of the happening on the bridge. "I was busy in the office and didn't hear the shooting — heard about it later. Otherwise I'd have been here sooner, knowing darn well you were mixed up in it somehow.

And that makes three you've nicked. Hmmm! You're slipping; should have meant three carcasses."

"We will live in hope," Slade smiled. The sheriff snorted and hammered for a refill.

"Ha!" exclaimed Amado. "The competition comes. It is the *Señor* Eldon Palmer, who bought the *cantina* on Callas Street the elderly Jose Gomez owned, who to retire wished. The place he made bright and shined. It attracts the younger men with whom he along well gets, listening to their problems, and to whom the advice he gives and, at times, when needed the helping hand. He says that those of the business alike should the — the sociable be and exchange views concerning business matters. So here he comes at times, and at times I him visit."

"An excellent attitude," Slade commented, regarding Palmer with interest.

The *cantina* owner was a tall and well-formed man with a straight featured face and keen-looking eyes. Slade

49

believed their color was light blue, although at that distance he could not be sure. His hair was dark, lightly sprinkled with gray. Between thirty-five and forty, Slade estimated his age.

Palmer found a place at the bar and ordered a drink, speaking a few words with the bartender who served him.

"I will him join for the moment," Amado announced, suiting the action to the word. Palmer smiled a welcome, and the two owners engaged in conversation.

"Nice lookin' feller," the sheriff observed. "Expect he'll make a go of it. Wouldn't be surprised if you could give him a few pointers, Dolores."

"Let Uncle Amado do the talking," Miss Malone replied with a shrug of their shapely shoulders. "After all, I'm just a dancing girl who is not supposed to know much except to try to keep from stepping on other people's feet and not get stepped on."

Slade regarded her with smiling eyes and, softly:

"O little feet, more white than
   snow,
If through the thorny brake ye
   go,
My loving heart I'll set below
To take the hurt for thee."

"There you go again!" she sighed.
"Yes, somebody, darn her, has been
teaching you to say pretty things."

"Just a quote I happened to recall,"
he replied.

"Uh-huh, you're always remembering
quotes you wrote yourself."

Slade decided it would be a waste of
time to try and argue the point. The
sheriff chuckled.

"I'm going on the floor for a while,"
Dolores said. "Try and keep out of
trouble till I get back."

Amado was still talking with Palmer,
so Slade and the sheriff had a chance
to converse without interruption.

"Well, have you learned anything?"
Calder asked.

"Not a thing," Slade replied.

"However, Estevan and his boys are circulating and may pick up something."

"After all," the sheriff commented, "you haven't been here quite twenty-four hours yet, and it isn't surprising that you haven't got the lowdown on things. Anyhow, you've had yourself quite a busy time of it and given three of the hellions something to remember you by. Which I figure ain't bad at all. All you need is a little time."

"Hope you're right," Slade answered.

"I ain't in the habit of being wrong," the sheriff declared. "I've watched you operate too many times to make a mistake. Let us drink."

Which they proceeded to do — Slade, coffee; the sheriff, a double snort.

"Was a rather smart try there on the bridge, wouldn't you say?" the sheriff observed meditatively.

"Yes, it was," Slade agreed. "Handled very adroitly. They would have known that, were I suspicious of them, I'd be watching them closely as they approached; whereas it was logical to assume after they had passed and were nearing the lip of the approach that my vigilance would be relaxed."

"Evidently didn't know *El Halcón* very well," the sheriff interpolated dryly.

"Possibly," Slade conceded. "It was not until they had passed me that I realized they had their heads turned from me, as if looking upstream, and that I never did get a really good look at their faces. That overhang of the bridge rail came in quite handy; I was practically out of sight when I went under it."

"Which I reckon they realized, too late," said Calder.

After a few final words with Amado, Eldon Palmer, the *cantina* owner, departed. His stride was lithe and vigorous. He wore a long black coat, a black string tie against the snow of his ruffled shirt front, a black 'J.B.' Rangeland riding boots, somewhat scuffed, struck a slightly incongruous note to his otherwise impeccable costume. Slade thought he had quite likely at one time been in the cattle business.

"Feller dresses sorta like a gambler is supposed to dress," the sheriff remarked.

"Many saloonkeepers do," Slade said. "A mark of the trade, as it were. Just as Amado wears a modified charro costume."

Amado had retired to his usual post near the till and the back room door. Calder moseyed to the bar to speak with acquaintances. Dolores rejoined Slade.

"And still the little house and the roses on Jackson Street?" he asked.

"Of course," she replied. "And they've both been lonely."

"You said that when I was here last," he reminded.

"Yes, and darn it! I meant it, just as I mean it now. Always they look toward the trail, the roses wafting their perfume in that direction, the house with two windows like wistful eyes."

"Nice of both of them," he commented. "And only the roses and the house?"

"Well — " She slanted him a glance through her lashes. They laughed together.

"Plenty of business tonight," he observed.

"Yes, there is," she agreed. "I'm going back on the floor for a while. Be seeing you, dear." She skipped off to the dance floor. Slade was left to relax comfortably with his coffee and cigarette.

5

LA LUZ was gay and colorful, but Slade was growing restless. Finally, he snuffed his cigarette and strolled out. For a while he wandered about through the bazaars and curio shops, studying faces, listening to snatches of conversation. He turned his steps toward the Casa Mata, on Calle B-2 and Camino a los Cemeterios, where there were numerous executions during the various revolutions. The old building always had a lonely, deserted look. Openings for rifle barrels pierced the second-story walls, and a large dome used as a lookout post rose above the flat roof.

The Casa Mata always held a certain fascination for Slade, perhaps because of its sinister history. Also, especially at night, it was avoided by many citizens of Matamoros, who believed it labored under a curse that could enfold the unwary. Slade had visited it and knew that on the second floor was a large hall, probably used as a meeting place in bygone days.

In back of the building was a spacious grove of very beautiful trees. He turned into Calle B-2 and walked slowly until he came to the grove. The high moon, shining through the widespread branches, formed a lovely filagree on the ground. Instinctively he turned into the grove and strolled along until he could see the back door of the building, which, to his surprise, stood more than a little ajar. It opened, he knew, onto a stairway that led to the second floor. However, the door was but a rectangle of blackness, and there was no light showing through the high windows. So he was still more surprised when he saw three furtive figures stealing across the open space between the grove and the building and vanishing through the partly open door. And as he stood wondering the why of those night prowlers, four more came into view to also enter the building, closely followed by still another four.

For several minutes *El Halcón* stood watching and listening; there were no further appearances. Who, he wondered, were those furtive night birds apparently foregathering in the 'haunted' structure? He waited a little longer; then, his curiosity at a white heat, he glided across the moon-dappled clearing to the door, hesitated a moment, then entered, mounting the steps on silent feet. To his ears came a low mutter of conversation.

He reached a point from where he could peer into the large meeting hall. There were benches, and on them were seated at least a dozen shadowy forms wearing an air of expectancy, or so he thought. What in blazes!

Standing utterly motionless, hardly breathing, Slade endeavored to catch a word or two of the low mutter, which was in Spanish.

From the foot of the stairs came

a scream, a horrible gurgling scream that cut off short. There was a thud of something falling.

Up the stairs hissed, "Come, *Captáin*! Quickly! Quickly!"

Whirling, Slade bounded down the stairs, leaped over a body lying sprawled across the sill to where Estevan loomed against the moonglow, shaking blood drops from his long blade. Together they sped across the clearing to the trees. They had barely reached them when a gun cracked and a bullet whined past. Slade whipped out both Colts and sent a stream of lead back toward the building. He aimed high, for he did not desire to kill anybody, just to discourage pursuit.

Evidently he did, for nobody crossed the clearing. He and Estevan raced through the grove to the far street, turned a corner and slowed down.

"My blade was swift, but I erred," said Estevan. "I hoped to kill at once, but twice I had to strike. You, *Captàin*, are all right?"

"Fine as frog hair," Slade replied. "How did you happen along as you did?"

"You I saw leave the *cantina*, and followed I," was the laconic reply. "You I saw enter that *casa* accurst. I followed and paused by the door, the shadow in, and saw that *ladrón* steal forward to follow you, gun in hand. I struck."

"You certainly did," Slade agreed. "And probably saved me from getting a slug in my back. What goes on, Estevan? What was that gathering in the hall?"

"*Capitàn*, I know not," the knife man answered. "But wager do I it was for good no."

"And I wager you are right," Slade said. "They were up to some hellishness. Appeared to be waiting for somebody."

"Doubtless to counsel evil give," said Estevan. Slade thought he was very likely right again.

"Well, I'd say you spoiled their meeting, for whatever purpose it was

60

being held," he said as he reloaded his guns. "There are other ways out of the Casa Mata, and I expect they used them. Well, across the street is La Luz. Coming in with me?"

"Outside I will wait for the while," Estevan decided.

"Okay," Slade replied. "And *gracias, amigo,* for everything."

"It was the privilege great," replied Estevan, bowing.

When Slade entered the *cantina,* Dolores, Amado, and the sheriff were at the table. The girl gave him an accusing look.

"Guns shoot we thought we heard," Amado said.

Slade told them exactly what happened. "Any idea what that gathering might mean, Amado?" he concluded.

The owner shook his head. "*Capitàin,* I know not. But nothing that is good, no doubt."

"You're darn right," growled the sheriff. "Trouble of some sort a-brewin'."

"When Estevan comes in, I'm going to kiss him," Dolores declared.

"And scare the life out of him," Slade predicted. "If there's anything he's afraid of, it's women."

"Perhaps, but I notice his eyes follow the girls on the floor," Dolores retorted. "It's late. I'm going to change."

"Doubt if the body found will be before it is day," commented Amado as he left the table. "There none of purpose good go while it is dark. It matters not."

Slade paid scant attention to his surroundings as, later, he and Dolores crossed the bridge and walked slowly along Jackson Street where the sheriff parted company with them. For he knew that Estevan and his knife men had cleared the way.

Early the following afternoon, Slade and the sheriff foregathered in the latter's office and discussed matters.

"What we've got to do now," the Ranger said, "is analyze the situation as it stands and endeavor to ascertain just where the bunch is likely to strike."

"So darn many things," growled Calder. "Trains, stagecoaches, banks, stores, rumholes, and Pete knows what else."

"Yes, there are," Slade agreed. "Suppose we start here for the present and work west. First we come to Santa Rita, just a few miles west of Brownsville, which back in the old days was the ranch home and headquarters of Cheno Cartinas, the Red Robber of the Rio Grande, as they called him, who actually once captured Brownsville and held it in thrall for forty-eight hours, looting and slaying. Not much to that pueblo any more, just a few old adobe shacks that appear to have always been there. Guess we can write off Santa Rita.

"Next to the west is La Paloma, very prettily named for a song, but not particularly melodious. Write it off, too. Then comes Los Indios, which began as a ranch. Several big ones in the vicinity now."

"And they all claim to have been losing stock," interpolated the sheriff. "Incidentally, there's a stage line from Los Indios to here. Comes down from Pharr, up to the north, and turns east on the river trail."

"Something to keep in mind," Slade said. "Also the widelooping angle. Santa Maria, seven or eight miles west of Los Indios, is also a mite hopeful, for there are pump irrigation and rich farmlands. Progresso, which belies its title, for there is little progressive about it, holds no interest.

"Now the trail bears close to the windings of the Rio Grande, and a couple of miles or so over to the river is Hidalgo. It will bear watching, for on the Mexican side of the river is the Mexican town of Teynosa, and there is little doubt but extensive smuggling is done there, with very often a lot of money changing hands. Our owlhoot *amigos* might sense opportunity there. We'll keep Hidalgo very much in mind.

"So, there's better than thirty miles

to the west covered as possibilities. Now you take over."

"Don't know where to start," grunted the sheriff. "There's the darn railroad from here to Port Isabel. And the stage line that comes down from Alice. That stage, and the one from Pharr, sometimes pack quite a hefty sum of *dinero*. Of course, the widelooping which has been going strong the past few months is something to think about, I'd say."

"Definitely," Slade agreed. "So all in all, looks like we have plenty of ground to cover. Our chore is to be at the right place at the right time."

"Oh, sure, that's all," snorted Calder. "Just as easy as all that. Well, you're pretty good at such a chore, so I ain't giving up hope. Think of past performance and feel better."

"Glad you're taking an optimistic viewpoint," Slade said smilingly. "Well, it isn't late, so I think I'll take a little ride west just for the fun of the thing. Might possibly spot something of interest; never can tell."

"Okay, but keep your eyes skun," advised Calder. "Somebody who figures you are of interest might spot *you*."

"I'll risk it," Slade laughed. "Be seeing you."

Getting the rig on Shadow, who, disliking being cooped up was in the mood for a leg-stretching, he set out through the gold of the Texas sunshine.

The little towns that lay ahead of him were like tarnished beads strung on a rusty wire, each being very much as the one before. He passed dilapidated Santa Rita, then drowsy La Paloma, then somewhat more lively Los Indios, and then Santa Maria, set in the prosperous-appearing farm belt. He had covered the twenty miles and more at a leisurely pace.

There followed a section of several miles where there were but a very few scattered farms. And now the trail dipped down near the river's edge, below the high bank. Slade knew he was passing over the Bar L spread owned by Dixon Lanham.

To the north, smoke fouled the clean blue of the sky. That smoke, he knew, came from the headquarters of the great irrigation project that the Alexander Company, a highly reputable concern that handled the projects to the east and west of Laredo, had under way. Slade smiled as he gazed at the smoke, for he was responsible for the project that employed several hundred workers at good wages.

Doubtless due to some terrestrial disturbance of past ages, the south section of Dixon Lanham's holding was lower than the land to the east and west. It was in the nature of a shallow and wide trough. Many, many years ago the Rio Grande, in times of high water, overflowed onto that lowland, overflowed and constantly deposited silt. As a result, the land under a rind of grass was amazingly fertile, needing only water to grow really magnificent crops.

In addition, north of the river there

was, untold centuries before, a small lake. But the river cut its channel deeper and deeper and built up its banks higher and higher in the course of the years. As a result, there was no longer an overflow, and the lake dried up. However, it left a large depression, a hollow that would provide a storage basin or reservoir for water impounded against seasons of drought. A made-to-order storage basin just waiting to be filled. It was a great advantage to have one already at hand, construction of impounding basins being a costly business.

Slade had called the unusual geological formation to the attention of Ernest Clark, chief construction engineer of the Alexander Company, who handled the Laredo projects. Clark, an old friend of Slade's, had at once recognized the possibilities of the terrain, and as a result the Alexander Company had paid Dixon Lanham a very large price for his bottom lands. And now the project was in full swing and would ultimately mean greater prosperity and more homes. *El Halcón* rode on, experiencing a quiet content.

Most of the Santa Maria shacks and farm houses were old, in many cases badly in need of repair. So he was somewhat surprised when, west of the little settlement, passing a line of flourishing grape arbors, he came upon a cabin that was either quite new or had undergone extensive repairs.

The land was fenced, and leaning on a gate post opposite the cabin was a man who waved a greeting. He was quite tall and broad, with a leather-looking, big-featured face. His eyes, Slade noted, were light blue and keen looking; his hair, dark but with a hint of being on the tawny side. His mouth was rather wide with thin lips.

"Howdy," he called. "Pull up and give your nag a breather."

Slade did so, smiling at the friendliness of the other's tone, although he knew he was being favored with a sharp look.

"Say!" the man exclaimed, "I thought

so. You're Mr. Slade, Sheriff Calder's deputy, ain't that right?"

"Guess it is," Slade conceded, "but you have the advantage of me."

"Soon remedy that," the other chuckled. "My handle is Ross, Mr. Slade, Taylor Ross. You were pointed out to me in the Blue Bell the other night; that's how I happened to know yours." He opened the gate, stepped out and held up a big hand, which Slade shook.

"If you can spare a little time, light off and come in for some coffee and a snack," Ross invited. "I bach it, but I'm a pretty good cook and can throw together a passable surrounding."

"Thanks, I will," Slade accepted. "I'm not headed for anywhere in particular; just taking a little ride. This brisk early autumn air sharpens one's appetite."

Which was true, and he was interested in a snack at the moment. But he was more interested in Taylor Ross, who, he felt, was something of a character.

"Got a little stable in the back where we can put your horse along with mine, and he can partake of a helpin' of oats to while away the time. Sure is a fine looking critter. Mind if I stroke him? I never touch another man's cayuse unless he gives me permission to."

"All right, Mr. Ross," Slade replied. "It's okay, Shadow."

"Hmmm!" said the other, "A one-man horse, eh? I like that kind."

He stretched out a fearless hand, and Slade was confident that Taylor Ross 'knew' horses.

Slade dismounted, and Ross led the way to a tight little stable back of the house and almost invisible from the road, where Shadow was domiciled in a stall next to one occupied by a very good looking red sorrel. Ross dumped a generous portion of oats into his manger.

"Guess that'll hold him until you're ready to amble," he remarked, and they headed for the cabin. Slade noted that Ross walked with a slightly rolling gait,

71

almost a swagger, with a heaving of his big shoulders.

"Don't recall seeing your place when I was in the section before," Slade remarked. "The arbors, yes, but not the house."

"I settled here only about three months back," Ross explained. "Bought the land from a farmer who wanted to move farther up the valley, where he has friends. There was an old adobe where the house now stands. Had the shack thrown together — rather roughly, I fear, but good enough for my purpose. Keeps out the wind and the rain and is comfortable. Yes, good enough for a man who lives alone. I have some Mexican boys working for me, but they go home at night. Left a mite early today — a fiesta to celebrate." He flung open the door, and they entered.

6

THE front room, which took up most of the cabin, was plainly but tastefully furnished. Three comfortable chairs, a table, and a couch under the windows. And, to Slade's surprise, a grand piano with age-mellowed ivory keys.

Lining one wall were shelves on which reposed a number of books. Slade noted works on forestry, farming, land conservation, irrigation, among others. Quite a few classical volumes and several dealing with music. It appeared that Mr. Ross was cosmopolitan in his choice of literature.

"Kitchen in the back and a little cubbyhole of a sleeping room," the host remarked. "Sit down and take it easy while I get busy on the snack. See you're looking over my books. Took quite a while to collect them.

73

A lot of valuable information there for one who hankers to be a progressive farmer."

"You've been in farming before, Mr. Ross?" Slade asked.

"Nope," was the reply. "My first try at it. Guess it's in the blood. My grandfather was a farmer, as was his father before him, over around El Paso way. Grew mostly grapes. I spent a lot of time with them.

"Dad, on the other hand, was a cattleman. Owned a small spread down toward the Malone Mountains. When he passed on, I inherited it. But somehow I could never cotton to the cow business, and I did like farming. So I sold the spread and figured to invest in farmlands. But as you know, land prices in the Middle Valley are sorta steep, and I didn't figure I had enough money to invest there. Had heard about this section and ambled over for a look-see. Decided this holding would be just right for me and figured to grow grapes — soil here is ideal for

74

them. So here I am. Now I'll get busy with the snack before we both topple over." He vanished into the kitchen, from whence came a sound of rattling cooking utensils.

While the snack was being prepared, Slade sat in the living room, smoking and thinking; his interest in Taylor Ross had increased, decidedly so.

An able and adroit man was his conclusion, apt to make a success at anything to which he turned his hand. A hard man, too, if aroused. His big-featured face, his rather tight mouth, and the glitter in his deep-set eyes evinced that. Yes, an interesting character.

In short order, his host called him to a very tasty meal and steaming coffee, to which both did full justice, after which they retired to the living room and an after-dinner smoke.

"See you've noticed my piano, too," Ross remarked. "I love music and just couldn't leave it behind; was my grandmother's instrument. Cost me a pretty penny to freight over here; but worth it."

"You play?" Slade asked.

"Oh, I paw at the keys a little," Ross replied, deprecatingly. "My big blunt fingers aren't exactly fitted for such work." He gazed at *El Halcón* a moment, then said, "The feller who pointed you out to me, one of Charge Grundy's cowhands, said folks called you the singingest man in the whole Southwest." He hesitated, then, his voice diffident: "Mr. Slade, I love music, and I'd take it mighty kind if you'd sing for me once before you go."

"With pleasure," the Ranger replied. In fact, he desired to learn just what effect music would have on his host. He crossed to the piano, adjusted the stool to his liking.

"You play, too?" Ross asked.

"A little," Slade replied. He sat down, ran his slender fingers over the keys with crisp power. The old instrument, a good one, boomed forth mellow chords. Ross straightened in his chair, his eyes widening.

Slade played a soft prelude, flung back his black head and sang!

Songs of the rangeland flooded with the gold of the Texas sun. Of the silvered dusk, the bonfire stars above. Of the intrepid riders who laughed at danger. Of the restless pioneers who, men and women, won the West. Of the farmer who tilled the soil that other men might eat, his old flintlock ever by his side. All in all, a very saga of Texas, and America.

And as his great golden baritone-bass pealed forth to fill the room with melody, his listener sat entranced.

The music ended with a crash of chords. And for some reason, across Slade's mind drifted the memory of another who had sat entranced while listening to his music — *El Cascabel*, the Mexican bandit leader who died in blood, taking a Texas bandit leader with him to the grave.

Taylor Ross's keen eyes were a trifle

misty, and his voice shook a little when he spoke. "Thank you, Mr. Slade, thank you," he said. "It was wonderful. I do love good music, and seldom do I have the good fortune to listen to any remotely compared with what you just rendered. Thank you!"

Slade glanced out the window at the flaming splendor of the sunset. "Guess I'll be moving," he said. "Isn't late, and my horse is rested. Think I'll ride on to Progresso and perhaps a little farther west before turning back. Promises to be a nice night, with a moon a little later, and I'm in no particular hurry to get back to Brownsville. Hope to see you again."

"And I certainly hope to see you soon again," replied Ross. "Please drop in some time."

Slade promised to do so.

Ross accompanied him to the stable and waved a final farewell as he rounded a bend in the trail. Slade rode on, feeling he had met with an intriguing experience; Taylor Ross was a man to give some thought to.

It was well past full dark when he reached Progresso, but he continued a few more miles before turning Shadow's head.

"Well, feller, homeward bound," he told the horse. "Folks will begin to think we got lost in the shuffle; so june along and try sifting a little sand for a change."

Shadow, who had already sifted quite a bit since noon, snorted derisively and quickened his gait a bit.

Ross's cabin was dark when they passed it, which was not remarkable; farmers were usually early to rise and early to bed. They also passed the thundering pump that lifted water from the river to irrigation ditches. Then quiet and dark Los Indios.

And now Slade rode watchful and alert, for it was a lonely trail at night and anyone met on it might be questionable, to put it mildly. He hardly thought that he had been followed out of town and his return route guessed, but best not to take chances. There were plenty of places suited for a drygulching, did some enterprising gentleman have one in mind.

Without misadventure, he made his way past La Paloma, which wasn't singing, not at this time of night. Ten miles to Santa Rita, then four more to Brownsville; should make it not too long past midnight.

It was a night of brilliant moonlight, another point in favor of the possible drygulcher. But it was the moonlight that saved the lone rider from disaster. Moonlight, and a trifle; but *El Halcón* had learned never to ignore or underestimate the importance of trifles.

Directly ahead, a couple hundred yards, the trail, which ran through a stand of chaparral, turned sharply, and from where Slade rode, he could see across the bend, over the tops of the lower growth on the west side. And the trifle appeared, at least to the eyes of *El Halcón*.

It was only the top of a tall bush swaying slightly. But why should a bush sway when there was not a breath of air stirring — sway as if somebody had stumbled or brushed against the slender supporting trunk! Slade instantly reined in and sat gazing toward the bush in question.

"May mean nothing at all," he breathed to Shadow, who stood silently and utterly motionless. "But then again, it could mean a great deal. Anyhow, I'm not going to ride past there without a mite of investigating. Guess a little polite snooping is in order. So into the brush with you, and keep quiet."

The maneuver was executed in perfect silence. Slade dropped the split reins to the ground, bestowed a pat on his mount's glossy neck and stole forward, circling to the north of the bend. He had marked the spot where stood the telltale bush that had warned him. Opposite it, he paused and stood motionless, straining ears and eyes.

It was his amazingly keen hearing that told him he had done the wise thing. Drifting through the growth came a low mutter of voices. Slade quickly concluded there were but two of the devils holed up, watching the trail to the west. He eased along a few more paces, then edged his way toward the trail. With the odds against him, it was all-important that he spot the drygulchers before they spotted him — spot them and rely on the element of surprise to react in his favor. He hesitated a moment, then glided forward a few more paces and saw the drygulchers.

But it was very dark under the spreading branches, and they were little more than shadows, certainly not good targets. Now he could hear what was said.

"When is he going to show?" a grumbling voice said. "Sure ought to have before now. I tell you, I don't like it; that big hellion is deadly."

"Take it easy," replied a second voice. "The boss said he'd sure be coming this way. We'll get him."

Silence followed. Slade stood motionless, hoping a name would be spoken. Minutes passed; then the first voice broke the silence, querulously, "When *is* the horned toad gonna show!"

"Gents," Slade called softly, "he has already showed!"

Startled exclamations. The shadows whirled. A gun blazed.

But *El Halcón* was ready. Before the report boomed out, he was crouched low behind a bush. He drew and shot with both hands.

A gasping cry echoed the reports, and a thud. Answering slugs whipped through the growth over his head, showering him with twigs. One just sliced the crown of his hat. He shot as fast as he could squeeze trigger — again, and yet again.

Abruptly he realized there was no more lead coming his way. He crouched motionless, hardly breathing, and heard nothing. Taking a chance, he surged erect, bounded forward and almost tripped over two bodies sprawled on the ground. A vagrant beam of moonlight piercing the growth fell on the hard-lined faces.

Guns ready for instant action, Slade waited. Neither form moved, and the pale shadow on the faces was the shadow of Death's passing wing.

Automatically, he reloaded his guns and stood listening. No sound broke the silence. The wan moonlight shone. The growth stood motionless. Slade holstered his guns and moved closer. He struck a match to augment the moonlight and scanned the faces of the pair; he had never seen either before. Well, their drygulching days were over. He leaned against a convenient tree trunk, rolled and lighted a cigarette, which he smoked slowly, reviewing the situation as it stood, wondering if somebody might come looking for the pair, possibly the mysterious 'boss' one had mentioned, and decided it was unlikely. Little sense in hanging around waiting.

Pinching out his cigarette butt, he browsed around and located the horses ridden by the drygulchers, tethered to a branch. Removing the rigs and tossing them aside, he turned the animals loose to fend for themselves.

Returning to where he had left Shadow, he mounted and resumed his interrupted amble to Brownsville, now only a half-dozen miles or so distant.

"Don't think we'll have any more excitement tonight," he told the horse. "But just the same, keep your eyes peeled and your ears to the front. The bunch operating hereabouts don't appear to play the game according to the rules, they make their own rules. So best not to take chances."

However, he finally reached Brownsville, some little time past midnight, without further mishap. Stabling Shadow and giving him a good rubdown and a generous helping of oats, he headed for the Blue Bell to put on the nosebag himself, it having been quite a while since the snack with Taylor Ross.

As he expected, he found the sheriff awaiting him.

"Well, you must have taken yourself quite a ride," Calder commented. "How come you got that hole through the top of your hat?"

"Cow put a horn through it," was the airy reply.

"Must have been some cow, to reach up that high," snorted the sheriff. "All right, let's have it."

"Well, you've been complaining about a lack of bodies to gloat over; so I figured I'd better supply you with a couple," Slade answered.

"What! What!" exclaimed the sheriff. "What you talkin'about?"

Slade told him, briefly. The sheriff said several things that wouldn't stand repeating.

"Hmmm! Sorta catchin' up with the devils at last, eh?" he concluded. "Not a bad bag — two. And counting the one Estevan did for makes three."

"If he was one of the bunch," Slade replied.

"Oh, he was, all right; no doubt in my mind as to that," Calder replied. "Okay, I'll ride over there come daylight and fetch the carcasses. Office floor will look more natural, with them laid out on it. Anything else happen?"

Slade mentioned his contact with Taylor Ross, the grape farmer from Arizona.

"Do you know him?" he asked.

"Oh, sorta," Calder said. "Comes in every now and then. Don't mix much and always behaves himself. Visits with Charge Grundy, I understand. 'Pears to be all right, wouldn't you say?"

"Yes, he appears to be," Slade conceded. The sheriff shot him a sharp look but did not comment.

While they were eating, a beat of hoofs sounded outside, halting at the hitchrack in front of the saloon. After a couple of minutes Dolores Malone entered.

"I knew you'd be stopping here first, and I didn't want you walking across that bridge tonight," she said to Slade.

"Nice and considerate of you," Slade replied. "Any particular reason why you didn't want me to walk across tonight?"

"No," she answered, "except that Estevan seemed a little excited about something. Said to tell you he'd see you tomorrow."

Slade looked decidedly interested; Estevan excited meant action somewhere before long.

"You've no notion what he was excited about?"

Again the answer was negative. "I doubt if anybody else noticed it," she added. "But I know his every mood, and the look in those glittery eyes of his told me he was. And what have you been mixed up in today?"

Slade told her, briefly, including his meeting with Taylor Ross. She sighed and shook her curly head resignedly.

"Always the same old story," she said. "You couldn't walk across the street without getting tangled up in something. Don't know how long I can take it."

"Don't bother about him," counselled the sheriff, a twinkle in his frosty eyes. "You know he always ends up on top."

"And that will be enough from you," Dolores told him.

"Yes, I'll have a small glass of wine."

The sheriff had another snort, Slade a last cup of coffee.

Calder remarked, "I'll round up the boys and head for the carcasses about noon. You going along?"

"Guess I might as well," Slade agreed. "Will save you hunting around in the bush for them."

"And if he doesn't mix you up in something, I miss my guess," Dolores declared.

"You're getting to be a pessimist," Slade smiled. "Come on, and I'll stable your horse for you."

7

SHORTLY after noon, Slade, the sheriff and the two deputies rode west, taking along a couple of pack mules to accommodate the bodies. Slade was watchful in the course of the ride, although he thought there was scant chance of a repeat performance so soon.

They found the bodies right where he left them, and, to all appearances, nothing had been disturbed. Nothing remarkable about either, so far as he could ascertain; typical border scum of the worst sort.

Their guns and their rigs were standard cowhand equipment. Their pockets divulged nothing save quite a large sum of money. "More than they'd ever tied onto from honest work," said Calder as he stowed it away.

Slade walked to where the horses had

been tethered the night before, then moved slowly toward the trail, carefully scanning the rather soft ground.

"What you see?" the sheriff asked curiously.

"Something rather interesting," the Ranger replied. "It would appear that if the pair rode out from town, they passed the point where they holed up, then turned and rode back to it before entering the brush, presumably after continuing west for a little ways. Or, which might seem a trifle illogical, they rode here from the west, and not from town."

"That *is* interesting," said Calder. "Any notion what it might mean?"

"Not the slightest, at the moment," *El Halcón* answered. "But I feel it's something to keep in mind, assuming as it does that they could have a hole-up somewhere to the west, which it would be to our advantage to ferret out."

"You're darn right," the sheriff agreed. "Might simplify matters greatly.

Well, guess there's nothing more we can do here; so might as well load up the carcasses and head back to town."

They proceeded. Again Slade rode watchful and alert, for it seemed certain puzzling angles to which he did not have the answer kept developing. It was slow going with the burdened mules, and sunset was already glowing in the west when they reached Brownsville, where the passage of the grim cortege through the streets quickly aroused quite a bit of excitement. By the time they drew rein at the sheriff's office, they had collected quite a following. Volunteers at once helped unload the bodies and place them on the floor.

"Look 'em over, and see if you can remember seeing the scuts before," Calder directed.

The results of the inspection that followed were vague and, Slade thought, of little value. Several citizens believed they had seen the pair hanging around town, but as to just where and under what circumstances they were not able to say. This was not particularly surprising, considering the constant goings and comings, with strangers attracting scant attention so long as they behaved themselves.

Calder hoped that some night bartenders who would show up later might prove more definite. After a while he shooed out the stragglers and locked the door. Deputy Webley fetched coffee from the stove in the back room, and they settled down to relax for a short time before heading to the Blue Bell and something to eat.

A tap sounded on the door. Calder opened it to admit Estevan. He accepted a chair and a cup of coffee and for some moments regarded Slade, who waited patiently; there was no rushing Estevan. At length the knife man spoke. "*Capitàn*", he said, "from a *cantina* by the river, thought not well of by the *alcalde* and the *jefe político*, two *hombres* came out. They mounted *caballos* and west rode by the Camino Real. Curious, I followed, my *caballo* being nearby. For the miles some past Santa Rita to where a ford is they rode. By the ford they crossed the river. I could see that on the Texas shore they turned west by way of the river trail. Across the river I did not follow, because of the moon bright; I would assuredly have been seen, which I felt was not good, to be seen riding on the trail of such."

"Could have been very bad," Slade concurred. "Did you recognize them?"

Estevan shook his head. "Their faces good I was never able to see," he replied. "They were men of the middle size, I would say. More I know not. I thought *Capitàin* should know, but learned he had from the town ridden. So I waited until today."

"I'm glad you told me," Slade said. "Could possibly mean something important. They might have been the two drygulchers, although not necessarily so, of course. Take a look at them over there on the floor and tell me what you think." He himself thought that things were getting more complicated all the time.

Estevan did as he was bid and again shook his head. "Those I have not seen before, so far as recall I. They seem to me to be the same size and build as the *hombres* I followed; that is all."

"May turn out to be plenty," Slade told him. "Keep an eye on that *cantina*."

"That I will do," the knife man promised.

"Chances are I'll have a look at it myself before long," the Ranger added. "See you in Amado's later."

Estevan finished his coffee and glided out. The sheriff speculated his departure.

"A plumb real *hombre*, that young jigger," he remarked. "Well, I'd like to run over and have a word with Doc McChesney, the coroner, before we eat. Line him up on the inquest he'll want to hold. Lock the door if you hanker to be let alone. Come along, Webley."

After Calder and the deputy left,

Slade sat for some moments gazing out the window. He drew pen, paper and ink from a drawer and wrote a brief letter that he addressed to Captain James McNelty, Ranger Post Headquarters.

"Maybe you'll tend to straighten out the tangle a little," he told the letter as he sealed and pocketed it. "Should get a reply within a couple of weeks at most; Captain Jim works fast."

The sheriff returned. "Doc will hold an inquest at two o'clock tomorrow afternoon, if nothing prevents," he announced. "Let's go."

They found the Blue Bell animatedly discussing the frustration and downing of the drygulchers, the consensus of opinion being that the blasted wind spiders were at last on the run.

"Told you when Mr. Slade got here that business would pick up; he's a go-getter from way back."

"Nice hearing, but I fear their optimism is a trifle premature," Slade remarked to Calder. "For the past few days the devils have been concentrating on me. Shortly, I predict, they'll turn to something else, probably with more success."

"Anyhow, they're getting a dose of what it means to buck *El Halcón*, and my money is still on *El Halcón*," the sheriff said cheerfully. "If I could tie onto any takers, I'd get rich. Let us eat!"

They had nearly finished their meal when the sheriff uttered an exclamation. "Hello! Here comes Amado's competition he mentioned the other night."

Slade had already noted the entrance of Eldon Palmer, the Matamoros *cantina* owner, who made his way to the bar not far from where Fats Boyer stood and ordered a drink.

"Big feller," Calder remarked. "Almost as tall as you and plenty wide across the shoulders. Wonder what he's doing here?"

"Possibly looking over *his* competition," Slade guessed. "I gathered from Amado that his place gets quite a few of the younger cowhands from over here. Wouldn't be surprised if he strikes up a conversation with Boyer."

However, it was Boyer who started the conversation, moving up the bar to welcome the newcomer to his establishment. Quickly they were talking together animatedly. Very likely, Slade thought, discussing the various angles of the saloon business.

This was proven to be the case a little later, when Palmer departed and Boyer joined Slade and the sheriff. "Feller knows his business, all right," he remarked, jerking his head toward the swinging doors. "'Pears to get along well with the Mexican boys, too. But I've a notion he'd like to open a place on this side of the river, if he can tie onto a location that suits him. I told him I'd look around a bit. Okay by me; the more the merrier."

"You don't need to worry about competition where this rumhole is concerned," grunted Calder. "All the plumb ornery rapscallions just nacherly flock here, after they've been thrown out of all the other places."

Boyer grinned at the obvious slander but refrained from arguing the point. "One on the house," he said. "Coffee for Mr. Slade, a snort for the sheriff. Rattle your hocks, waiter, we have to take care of our rapscallions."

"Incidentally, Palmer was quite interested in you, Mr. Slade. Said he's glad that at last somebody can make headway against the outlaws. Says they're bad for business, which they are, of course. Everybody knows that."

"And I fear *he* also is a trifle premature in his conclusion," Slade replied smilingly. "I haven't made much headway yet, so far as I can see; just managed to keep alive for a while."

"Uh-huh, but you've done more in a coupla days than anybody else has in months," declared Boyer.

Said the sheriff, sententiously, "My money is still on *El Halcón*. Let us drink!"

After he finished his snort, he asked, "Now what's in order?"

"I think I'll ride across to Matamoros," Slade replied. "May learn something over there."

"Okay," agreed Calder. "And if you don't mind, I'm going to bed; feel sorta tuckered. Very little sleep last night. Was a lot of paper work that's been piling up in the offices; so I got up early to take care of it before settin' out for the carcasses."

"A good idea," Slade said, pushing aside his empty cup. "See you tomorrow."

Saying goodnight to Boyer, he made his way to the stable and cinched up.

"Just have a sort of hunch, horse, that we may end up doing a bit of ambling tonight," he said. "Don't know why, but I feel that way."

Shadow snorted cheerful agreement and stepped out at a brisk pace. They crossed the bridge without incident. Slade left Shadow at the rack in front of La Luz, with a nosebag of oats to keep him occupied, and entered the *cantina*, which was busy and rather more noisy than usual, with quite a few Texas cowhands present, who tended to enliven things.

Dolores waved to him from the floor; Amado from the far end of the bar. Slade settled himself comfortably, ordered coffee and awaited developments — which were not too long in coming.

A little later, Dolores skipped over from the dance floor and plumped into a chair beside him. "Just got a minute to stay," she said. "A lot of work to do in the back room, but I'll be with you after a bit. Try and not get mixed up in something."

He promised, but experienced a feeling that he wouldn't be able to keep the promise; the hunch was strengthening.

Only a few minutes had passed when Estevan glided in and occupied the chair Dolores had vacated, his eyes glittering.

"*Capitán*," he said without preamble,

"this night I again that *cantina* of repute not good watched. From it came three men whose looks I liked not. *Si*, I would recognize them did they I again see. They outside paused and in every direction looked, but saw not I who was in a dark doorway hidden. I heard one say, 'Okay, everything looks in the clear.' What they meant I know not. *Caballos* they mounted and rode, not by the Camino Real, but across the bridge. My own *caballo* was nearby and I, much curious, also rode. In Brownsville they stopped not but rode on. Outside of the town they turned into the old trail, hardly ever ridden now, that the railroad beside runs. In no hurry they seemed, for slowly they rode, talking. What was said I could not hear. I thought *Capitán* should know and turned back, swiftly riding."

For several moments Slade sat silent, digesting what the knife man had told him. He was familiar with the almost-never-used trail in question. In the beginning it had serviced the railroad from Boca Chica to Palmito Hill that General Philip H. Sheridan built in 1865 and had been continued as part of the contemplated project to Brownsville. It had been abandoned when Maximilian, the French invader, withdrew his forces from northern Mexico, and the threat of war dissipated. What reason had the three men for riding that deserted track? Slade asked himself the question, but didn't have the answer — yet.

"How long since they rode?" he asked Estevan.

"The perhaps little than the hour more," the knife man replied.

Again Slade sat silent for a couple of minutes; he was beginning to get an idea.

The first commercial railroad was built from Brownsville to Point Isabel in 1870, the route following closely the old trail laid out by Sheridan's engineers.

Slade broke his silence after a glance at the clock. "Estevan," he said, "go back to that *cantina* and keep watch; perhaps you may be able to learn something more."

Estevan nodded and glided out. The chore would keep him occupied for a while. Slade knew that if he told the knife man what he had suddenly resolved to do, he would wish to accompany him, and *El Halcón* believed he could handle the chore better alone, even with the odds of three-to-one against him. For one thing, he would have to do some very fast travelling for a while, and Estevan's mustang would not be able to keep up with Shadow.

Dolores was still in the back room; Amado, busy at the far end of the bar. Slade left the *cantina* without attracting the attention of either.

Reaching the rack, he flipped off Shadow's nosebag, set the bit into place, mounted and headed for Brownsville at a fast pace, passing through the almost deserted streets without interruption. Outside town, he turned into the old track, grass-and weed-grown, and rode east by south.

"It's a *loco* hunch, feller, but we're going to play it," he told the horse. "I think the devils are going to make a try for the night passenger train, which sometimes packs a hefty passel of *dinero*. And I'm pretty sure I know just about where it will be pulled, if it is. I think we can make it in time, for they won't start placing the obstruction on the track until almost train time; sometimes a freight precedes the passenger, and they wouldn't want to wreck that. Yes, I think we can make it." His voice rang out, clear, compelling: "Trail, Shadow, trail!"

The great black lunged forward and in a matter of seconds was going at top speed, spurning the earth with his pounding irons.

Slade constantly scanned the trail ahead. The point he had in mind was where the railroad right-of-way, running between tall chaparral, curved sharply and was quite a little lower down than the trail, with the growth bristling up to conceal a rider following the track from the west. He believed the wreckers would be so concentrating on the business at hand that they would not detect his approach. If they did and waited for him, what subsequently happened would hold no interest for him. Nor would anything else on this earth, for that matter. That, however, was the chance he had to take, with the moon plenty bright to provide excellent shooting light for gentlemen holed up in the brush.

On and on raced the tall black horse without slackening speed, showing no signs of exhaustion, the miles flowing back under his flying hoofs.

As he rode, Slade began to grow anxious. It appeared he had under-estimated the distance he had to cover. And then he saw the spot in question, less than a quarter of a mile distant. Sitting tense in the saddle, his eyes roving back and forth across the growth, he calculated the shrinking space between him and the curve and curbed Shadow. A couple of hundred yards more and he drew rein; couldn't risk a nearer approach on horseback. Slipping to the ground, he eased his mount into the chaparral, which effectively concealed him, and with quick, light steps sped forward on foot. Almost at the apex of the railroad curve below, he entered the growth and drifted silently toward the tracks. His pulses leaped exultantly as to his ears came a mutter of voices and a thudding and scraping sound.

And at that moment, faint with distance, sounded a mellow whistle note!

Flinging caution to the winds, Slade dashed forward and into the open. Approaching the tracks were three men, each carrying a heavy crosstie for the obstruction that would wreck the approaching train.

"Up!" Slade shouted. "In the name of the State of Texas, you are under arrest!"

The ties thudded to the ground. The outlaws went for their guns. Slade drew and fired. One wrecker fell. Bullets stormed past the weaving, ducking Ranger. One just grazed his elbow, throwing him off balance for an instant. He recovered, shot right and left. A second man plunged forward onto his face. As Slade squeezed both triggers, the remaining wrecker fired with deadly aim.

A jagged flame roared up from earth to heaven. The whole breadth of the sky seemed torn asunder. Black darkness swooped down, fold on clammy fold.

The train from Point Isabel rumbled past, exhaust chuckling, side rods clanking. The red rear markers winked out in the distance. The moon crossed the zenith; the stars changed position as the great clock in the sky wheeled westward. And in the shadow of the rails, four bleeding forms lay without sound or movement.

8

WHEN Walt Slade recovered consciousness, he realized he must have been unconscious for quite some time. He was wet with dew, shivering with cold; his head, a dull, monotonous ache. For moments he lay staring upward with unseeing eyes.

Gradually some of the fog drifted from his brain, and he essayed a sitting position. Pain stabbed, nausea enveloped him. For more minutes he sat holding his throbbing head in his hands, until the pain abated somewhat, and the cloying sickness passed. His mind was again functioning something like normal. He glanced at the three outlaw bodies sprawled nearby; nothing more to fear from them. He raised a shaking hand to his head and discovered a light, ragged furrow just below the hairline and above his right temple. He probed the area of the wound with his sensitive fingertips and concluded that, aside from the tremendous shock of the glancing bullet, he suffered no serious injury.

Abruptly he felt a lack. His guns! Groping about, he retrieved them, reloaded the big Colts with trembling fingers and sheathed them. Then, he managed to roll and light a cigarette. A couple of deep drags and he felt a lot better. The pain was almost gone, his mind clear.

But it had been touch-and-go. An inch to the left, and it would have been curtains. Lucky, too, that he had been able to do for the devil before he passed out; could have expected scant mercy at his hands.

Taking a chance, he stood up, found he was fairly steady on his feet. A whistle brought Shadow, snorting his utter disgust with the whole affair.

"Never mind," Slade told him. "I know you got tired of waiting, but you had it easier than I; didn't get your head cracked." Shadow refused to comment.

Securing his jar of antiseptic ointment from his saddle pouch, Slade smeared the wound and decided it needed no further attention at the moment. After all, it was little more than a deep cut, and the bleeding had long since stopped.

Browsing about in the brush, he located the three outlaw horses, removed the rigs and turned them loose. By the wan moonlight, aided by a couple of matches, he examined the dead wreckers and could note nothing outstanding about them. Typical hard-case guns-for-hire brand, on a par with the pair laid out in the sheriff's office. He didn't feel up to the chore of examining the contents of their pockets. Calder could take care of that later. With a glance at the crossties taken from a pile somewhere nearby, plain evidence of the intent to wreck the train, he mounted and headed for town. His head no longer ached; his strength had returned. Altogether, not such a bad night, he felt. May have very well prevented a few killings, and if the express car packed money, that had been saved. Little doubt but that it did, the outlaw bunch presumably learning about it in advance; seemed there was nothing they were not able to learn. Not too hard for a prominent property owner, which was something to keep in mind.

Dawn was flushing the eastern sky when he reached Brownsville. After caring for Shadow, he headed for the Blue Bell, where lights were still burning. He was not at all surprised to find Dolores Malone and Estevan awaiting him, Fats Boyer and Deputy Webley keeping them company.

Dolores gave a little cry and ran to him. "Oh, darling, you're hurt!" she whimpered.

"Just a scratch." Slade deprecated the injury.

"Scratch nothing!" she retorted. "You're blood all over. To the back room with you. If you won't take care of yourself, I'll do it for you."

Too tired to argue, Slade let her have her way. She sponged off the dried blood, padded and bandaged the wound.

"Now tell us what happened to you," she said.

Slade told them briefly. "So, you see, what you learned was really important," he told Estevan.

"But *Capitàn* should have I taken with him," the knife man said.

"I would have, except I knew I had no time to spare, and you couldn't have kept up with Shadow," Slade explained.

"I'll tell Calder as soon as he gets up, which will be soon; he's an early bird," Webley promised. "I already slept some tonight — turned out because I was hungry. Chances are he'll want to hustle over there right away and pick up the carcasses. I know where that place is; won't have any trouble finding it."

"Thanks," Slade said. "That will help. And now I'm going to call it a night."

★ ★ ★

When Slade reached the sheriff's office an hour or so past noon, he found Calder complacently regarding the bodies already laid out on the floor.

"You're darn right there was a hefty passel of *dinero* in that express car," he replied to a question. "A consignment to the bank to swing some sort of a deal. The railroad people are sure worked up over what you did, and so is everybody else, for that matter. Wonder how the sidewinders learned the money was in the car last night? Was supposed to have been kept quiet."

"I'd like to have the answer to that," Slade replied. "However, while such things are supposed to be secret, they seldom are."

114

"Those devils had quite a bit of money on 'em," Calder added, jerking his head toward the bodies. "Not so much as the others — vingaroons may be gettin' a mite short of spending money — but a good deal. I slipped some to Estevan; figured he earned it."

"He did," Slade said.

"We picked up the rigs and the horses, too," Calder resumed. "Good-looking critters, and should bring a sizeable price. Think the brands might mean something to you?"

"Not likely, but I'll take a look at them," Slade answered.

"Agosto has them at his stable," the sheriff said. "By the way, Taylor Ross, the grape farmer, was in asking for you. Sure 'pears to have taken a shine to you. Couldn't stop talking about your singing. I still think he's a sorta nice feller."

"He certainly gives that impression," Slade agreed.

Calder seemed to sense the non-committal inflection, for, as before when Taylor Ross was discussed, he bent the Ranger a sharp look, but again he did not comment.

"Well, Doc will be here with his coroner's jury to hold an inquest on the whole kit and caboodle in about an hour," he said. "Suppose you'll wait?"

"Seeing as I am the only witness in both instances, I guess I'd better," Slade smiled. "Hope he doesn't order me thrown in the calaboose."

"If he does, I'll chase him till he discovers a new street," the sheriff vowed. "Reckon you don't hafta worry, though. He sure thinks well of you. Says the doctorin' profession lost a mighty good man when you turned to — something else. Just as such big fellers as General Manager Jaggers Dunn of the C. & P. Railroad system, former Governor Jim Hogg, and Bet-a-Million Gates of Wall Street say the engineering profession lost one of the best engineers that ever rode across Texas when you turned to — something else."

116

There was truth in the sheriff's remark. Shortly before the death of his father, which occurred after financial difficulties that caused the loss of the elder Slade's ranch, young Walt had graduated with high honors from a noted college of engineering. He had hoped to take a postgraduate course in certain subjects to round out his education and better fit him for the profession he planned to make his life work.

That, however, became impossible at the moment, and Slade lent an attentive ear when Captain Jim McNelty, with whom Walt had worked some during summer vacations, suggested that he come into the Rangers for a while and pursue his studies in spare time.

So Walt Slade became a Texas Ranger. Long since, he had gotten more from private study than he could have hoped for from the postgrad and was eminently fitted for the profession of engineering. But meanwhile, Ranger work had gotten a strong hold on him. It provided so many opportunities for righting wrongs, suppressing evil, helping the deserving and making the land he loved a better land for good people. He was loath to sever connections with the illustrious body of law-enforcement officers. He was young and had plenty of time to be an engineer. He'd stick with the Rangers for a while longer.

And this was perhaps just what canny old Captain Jim expected to happen.

"How's your head feel?" the sheriff asked.

"I'd already forgotten all about it when I got in last night, but Dolores made a fuss over it and insisted on tying it up," Slade replied.

"Gal has sense," Calder grunted. "I'll fetch us some coffee."

They were smoking and sipping when, a little later, old Doc rolled in with his coroner's jury and held a decidedly informal inquest, the verdict justifying Slade, commending him on a good chore and expressing the hope that he'd soon bring in some more blankety-blank-blanks to be sat on.

"Now what's lined up?" the sheriff asked, after the coroner and the jury had departed in quest of refreshment.

"I think I'll browse around a bit," Slade replied. "Feel in a notion of looking things over. Meet you at the Blue Bell around nosebag time."

"Okay," Calder said. "Keep your eyes skun. Not much doubt but you're mighty unpopular in certain quarters about now."

Slade promised to do so and sallied forth into the sunshine. Although he believed there was little likelihood of anything being attempted against him so soon and in broad daylight, he did not take the sheriff's warning altogether lightly. He knew he was up against a shrewd, ruthless and resourceful bunch with a genius for the unexpected. And, it appeared, until his advent on the scene, the outlaws had been having things very much their own way. They would hardly take kindly to having that pleasant state of affairs abruptly terminated.

However, if something was planned, it was not put into execution. The afternoon passed peacefully, and dusk found Slade at the Blue Bell awaiting the sheriff, who arrived shortly.

"Learn anything?" he asked as he sat down and hammered for service.

"Not a thing," Slade replied. "Had a nice stroll and dropped in at a few places, including Burley Sturm's Last Chance. Teresa, his wife, Dolores' aunt, was there, per usual. Had a pleasant chat with them. They're keeping their eyes open and may come up with something of interest; the Last Chance gets all sorts."

"So does this rumhole," growled the sheriff, surveying the crowded and busy room with disapproval. "Hellions here I've never seen before and hope I'll never see again."

"I fear you're prejudiced," Slade said smilingly. "Or envious of Fats, who's getting rich."

"He can have it!" snorted Calder. "I prefer less money and less headaches; I've got enough of them as it is. Here comes my snort; about time. All set to eat?"

Slade was, and soon they were putting away a hefty surrounding of the cook's choice offering.

After they finished eating and enjoyed an after-dinner smoke, the sheriff remarked, "Suppose you're crossing the bridge tonight?"

"Yes, I think I will," Slade replied.

"And I'm traipsin' right along," Calder declared. "You ain't to be trusted alone. I'm still wondering if you had that ride in mind last night when you sent me to bed."

"No, I didn't," Slade replied. "I had nothing definite in mind until I talked with Estevan and he told me of those three hellions riding the railroad trail."

"I'm still suspicious," said the sheriff. "Okay, I'm ready to go if you are."

When they entered La Luz, they at

once spotted a familiar face. Taylor Ross was at the bar, conversing with half-a-dozen young Mexicans who were grouped about him, glasses in hand. He waved a greeting. The Mexicans bowed low to *El Halcón*.

"Come on over and squat and have a snort," the sheriff called.

"Don't mind if I do," Ross accepted. "And I want to congratulate Mr. Slade on what happened last night. Was a fine piece of work, and I'm mighty glad you escaped serious injury.

"Brought my boys with me tonight," he added, gesturing to the Mexicans. "They like it here, and they like to have the *patrón*, as they call me, drink with them. Work better because of it. I've learned that if you treat them as human beings and don't lord it over them, you get the best results."

Slade was heartily in agreement.

"And they sure think well of you, Mr. Slade," he resumed. "They bow their heads as to a shrine whenever your name is mentioned."

"Which is very, very nice of them,"
Slade said soberly. "I hope I'll always
be able to justify their regard."

"You will," Ross declared cheerfully.
"No doubt in my mind as to that. Say,
I also heard about those devils trying to
drygulch you the night you were riding
home after visiting with me. Mighty
glad that turned out as it did, too."

"I sort of feel that way about it
myself," Slade smiled. Ross chuckled,
and beckoned a waiter. A little later
he shoved his empty glass aside and
returned to his men, promising to
drop over again before leaving. Slade
watched him roll to the bar, sighed
resignedly and shook his head.

Dolores joined them and accepted a
chair and a small glass of wine, which
she sipped daintily.

"I like him," she said, nodding
toward Ross. "He's the big wooly
bear type, but he dances well and is
courteous and considerate. All the girls
are fond of him. And when he brings
his men in, it's not boss and workers;

he's just one of the boys. He's a good man."

"Yes, I fear he is," Slade sighed. Dolores glanced at him questioningly, but he did not elaborate.

Ross paused for a few minutes of talk before leaving. With a smile for Dolores and a word for Amado, he strode out. His men, nodding and bowing, filed after him. Business was rather slack, and everybody called it an early night.

9

SEVERAL quiet days followed. It appeared the outlaws were laying low for a spell. Or, perhaps, as the sheriff suggested, their recent manpower losses had given them a jolt from which they were slow in recovering.

"Whoever's heading the hellions may have all of a sudden found himself sorta short of hired hands," he observed.

Anyhow, there were no reports of depredations committed on either side of the river.

Slade, however, did not find this reassuring. He experienced an uneasy premonition that the outlaws were just biding their time, awaiting opportunity, and when they did strike, they would strike hard.

He received an answer to the letter

he wrote Captain McNelty sooner than he expected. It was laconic:

'Fellow tells a straight story. His grandfather and great grandfather were farmers. His father owned a small cow factory not far from the Malone Mountains, as he said. He enjoyed an excellent reputation in *El paso* and the Middle Valley.'

"And out the window goes my only anything-like-definite suspect," Slade said as he tossed the missive to Calder, who read it with knitted brows.

"Just who is old Jim referring to?" he asked.

Slade smiled wryly, and said, "*Taylor Ross!*"

"By gosh!" exclaimed the sheriff. "I had a notion you were looking sorta sideways at that jigger."

"I was, in a way, especially when it appeared those two devils who tried to drygulch me on the river trail apparently rode from the west," Slade conceded. "Ross knew I'd be riding for Brownsville later that night, and I didn't think anybody else did. In which I was evidently mistaken. I'll admit I became a trifle dubious after Estevan told me of those two men fording the river some miles west of Santa Rita and continuing west. I was pretty sure they were the drygulchers. Looked like they overshot their mark and turned back to reach the point where they planned the killing to take place. Either that or they had a hole-up some place west of Santa Rita where they waited until they figured I was about due to show. Which is interesting."

"You're darn right, especially if we could find it," said Calder. "So Ross is definitely out as a suspect."

"He was just about definitely out after that night we spent with him in La Luz," Slade replied. "Dolores liked him; Amado liked him; the dance floor girls liked him; and his workers showed plainly they were ready to fight for him at the drop of a hat. I certainly didn't give him credit for being smart enough to fool all those people, especially those of the feminine persuasion."

"And there's nobody left to tie onto?"

"About the size of it," Slade admitted. "I've been employing the trial-and-error method, studying everybody I've met who might possibly qualify as a suspect, and so far eliminating one after another. I think tonight I'll pay a visit to that *cantina* by the river where it's pretty certain some members of the bunch hang out. Might be able to learn something."

"Hadn't I better go along?" Calder offered.

Slade shook his head. "I believe I'd have a better chance to accomplish something alone," he declined. "If the sheriff of the county walks in, any off-color gentleman will be on the *qui vive* at once."

"Whatever the devil that means," growled the sheriff. "Okay, though, if you think best."

It was well past full dark when Slade and the sheriff rode across the bridge. *El Halcón* was very much on the alert during the course of the ride, but they reached Matamoros without incident of any sort, left their horses at the rack and entered La Luz, which was gay and colorful as usual.

Dolores joined them at once. "Had your dinner?" she asked.

"Nope; I'm feeling mighty lank," returned the sheriff.

"Take care of it right away," she said and trotted to the kitchen.

While they were waiting to be served, Estevan drifted in, paused at the end of the bar and shook his head; evidently he had nothing to report. Slade's resolve to visit the *cantina* by the river strengthened. *El Jabalino*, Estevan had mentioned it was called.

Why, Slade wondered, had it been named for a wild pig. For javelina was a wild pig, a vicious and dangerous little critter, especially when he travelled in packs. Then even the hardy *vaqueros* gave that particular *puerco* a wide berth, the only place safe from him being a tall tree.

Amado came over and chatted with them while they ate, then returned to his usual position. When they had finished eating, Slade and Dolores had a couple of dances together, after which she hied herself to the back room, where she had paper work to catch up with. Slade and the sheriff sat smoking and talking for a while, until *El Halcón* said, "Now, I'm going to make a try for that *cantina* with a pig's name and see what's what."

"And watch your step," cautioned Calder.

"Don't worry," Slade replied carelessly. "Estevan and his boys won't be far off."

He had no trouble locating Javelina, as he chose to call the saloon. It proved to be somewhat smaller than La Luz, the lighting not particularly good, and it was surprisingly quiet.

While he sipped a drink at the bar, Slade decided that the dubious title was not too much of a misnomer. The patrons, the majority of them, were hard-lined characters from both sides of the river. The place was clean, though, and the dance floor girls not bad. Nor was the orchestra, which played muted music.

Nevertheless, a sinister air pervaded, and Slade did not marvel that the *alcalde* was toying with the notion of closing the place. However, he had learned from experience that such an atmosphere did not necessarily mean a forerunner of violence and that sometimes the mild-appearing establishment was the more fraught with danger.

Just the same, though, he quickly concluded the place was packed with potential dynamite. Of the truth of this he was quickly to become aware.

Standing next to him were four men who had been paying him close attention from the moment he entered.

He saw their heads, reflected in the back bar mirror, draw together. He was not at all surprised when the man standing beside him jostled him rudely and snarled, as he drew back the glass he held, "Out of my way, you blankety-blank range tramp!" His companions crowded behind him.

Rows were common in Javelina, but not the kind of a row *El Halcón* kicked up that night. He well knew that under such circumstances an offense is the best defense. Without an instant's hesitation, he hit the glass-holder, hurling him back against the other three. And before they could recover from the unexpected assault, he was all over them, hitting with both hands. In a moment he had all four on the floor.

But they didn't stay there. They surged to their feet, spitting blood and curses and splintered teeth, and Slade knew the odds were too great. These devils were tough and could take plenty. Another moment and *he*

132

would be on the floor, the life kicked out of him. He leaped back, a flicker of movement, and the rushing quartette found themselves looking into the black muzzles of two long guns that had just 'happened' in Slade's hands. His great voice rolled in thunder through the room. "Hold it! I don't want to kill you, but make another move, and I will!"

And even as he spoke, he realized he was no longer alone. Flanking him, two on either side, were four dark-faced, glitter-eyed young men, long throwing blades swinging by the points.

A corpulent individual who was doubtless the owner came waddling forward, glaring at Slade.

"You!" he yelped. "You started this! I'll — "

"*Die!*" hissed Estevan, his knife flinging up to the throwing position.

The owner took one look and with a squall of fear scuttled back the way he had come. Slade holstered his guns and regarded the bloody, battered and decidedly crestfallen erstwhile trouble-makers, and his eyes were the eyes of *El Halcón*. They cringed under that icy stare.

"All right, back to the bar," he told them. "Don't try anything like that again, and thank your lucky stars you're still alive."

As they sullenly obeyed, he swept the suddenly silent room with his gaze.

"And if anybody else is in the notion of fanging, get goin," he said. "I aim to accommodate."

Nobody accepted the invitation.

"We'll have a drink and then amble back to La Luz," Slade told the knife men.

As he raised his glass, Estevan spoke, his lips moving not at all, his voice carrying only to Slade's ears. "What think you, *Capitán*; was it the plot to kill?"

"Frankly I don't know; it looked a little that way," Slade replied. "But then again it may have been just pure cussedness on their part. They were about half drunk, and they have the look of born trouble-hunters."

"Trouble they found," Estevan observed sententiously. "Wish I that even more they had found; my blade is thirsty."

"I fear it always is," Slade smiled. "However, I preferred there would be no killings, unless we were forced to kill, Better that way on this side of the river."

"It is so," Estevan agreed. But Slade noted that he took a long look at the four trouble-makers; he would know them, did he see them again.

Finishing his drink, Slade turned his back on the discomfited quartette and sauntered out. Estevan, however, walked with his chin on his shoulder, the long knife still in his hand. Not until they were through the swinging doors did he sheath it.

Without further mishap, they made their way to La Luz. Estevan and his men did not enter at the moment. but silently melted into the crowd that thronged the street. Slade had a very good notion that they were heading back to the neighborhood of Javelina to keep a watch on the trouble-hunters and learn what their possible movements might mean.

10

DOLORES was on the floor, Amado at the far end of the bar; the sheriff sitting alone, fortified with a full glass. Slade sat down and told him exactly what happened.

"And do you think it was another try at getting rid of you?" Calder asked.

"As I told Estevan, I don't know for sure, but I am of the opinion that it probably was," Slade replied. "If so, it was quite cleverly handled. One word leads to another; there is a row; and somebody, unfortunately, gets killed; an old trick. With a number of witnesses to swear I was the aggressor." He paused a moment, then added thoughtfully, "I've a notion that somebody, a very cunning somebody, figured that sooner or later curiosity would lead me to the place, which it did. So they had their little trap nicely set. But I caught them a mite off balance by getting into action before they did. Very fortunate, incidentally, that I had things pretty well under control before Estevan and his boys arrived. Otherwise somebody would still be packing bodies out. If I had happened to be down on the floor at the moment, they would have killed everybody they could reach."

"Wouldn't want you to have been down on the floor, but it's a pity Estevan and his boys didn't get into action," the sheriff growled. "Would have rid the earth of a lot of scum it could do without."

"Yes, but it would have posed problems for our old *amigos*, the mayor and the chief of police," Slade pointed out. "For they would be taking the law in their own hands, no matter how justified their acts. I could possibly get by, for I still hold the commission in the *rurales*, the Mexican mounted police, that the Governor of the state of Chihuahua granted me some years

138

back. However, I prefer not to display it, if possible. Better to be thought of over here as *El Halcón*."

"I suppose so," the sheriff conceded. "Anyhow your *El Halcón* reputation pays off on both sides of the river, even though it does lay you open for trouble."

"The right kind of trouble is nothing to bother about," Slade answered cheerfully.

"And here comes your 'trouble' right now," said Calder as Dolores skipped across from the dance floor. "Rather nice trouble, though, I hafta admit. Wine for the lady, waiter."

"Here comes Mr. Palmer," Dolores remarked, sipping her wine.

"Do you like *him*, too?" Slade asked.

The girl hesitated a moment. "Frankly, I don't, and for no apparent good reason," she replied. "Only, I'd say, because he always appears to adopt a superior attitude. Nothing offensive, but I sense it, and I don't think any woman likes to be looked down on."

"I would say you have the right of it there," Slade said, regarding the *cantina* owner's broad back with interest. Palmer's bearing was arrogant. Sufficient unto himself, Slade catalogued him. Accustomed to success and impatient with failure. This attitude could be a weakness. 'Never underestimate,' says the 'book,' not a printed book, of the Rangers. 'You may be making a serious mistake.'

With something like to a shock, he abruptly realized he was regarding Eldon Palmer as an opponent! Why? He was hanged if he knew. There certainly seemed no valid reason for doing so. Perhaps Dolores' remark was at the bottom of it. Could be, for he had learned to rely on her judgment, especially where men were concerned.

The whole conclusion was manifestly absurd, but once such a train of thought is started, it is difficult to sidetrack it. Slade began paying particular attention to Eldon Palmer.

To all appearances, Palmer was not

armed. His swungback coat revealed no holster or cartridge belt. But when he dropped his arm onto the bar, Slade's amazingly keen ears caught a tiny thud. Without doubt, Palmer was a sleeve-gun man carrying the wicked little double-barrel, forty-one caliber derringer that a jerk of the wrist would spit into the wearer's palm.

Slade's equally keen eyes also detected a very slight bulge just to the right of the left armpit of the otherwise meticulously fitting long black coat. Palmer wore a second gun in a shoulder holster; the *cantina* owner was prepared against any emergency.

Still, it meant little in the final analysis. Palmer had quite probably been a gambler or a card dealer at some time or other, and such arms were the standard equipment of those gentry.

"Next thing I know, I'll be seeing blue snakes with pink tails," the Ranger chuckled to himself and turned his attention back to Dolores. The whole activity of discovery and deduction had consumed but a matter of seconds.

"Say, what have you been into?" the girl asked. "Your knuckles are bruised, and one is bleeding a little."

He told her, in detail, for there were no secrets between them. She shook her curly head resignedly, as had been a habit with her of late.

"Well, I'm glad it was no worse," she said.

"It might have been had not Estevan and his boys been right there to back my play," he replied. "They are real *amigos*, and utterly dependable."

"Yes, they are all of that," she conceded. The sheriff nodded vigorous agreement.

"All right, I'll fetch some salve and smear that cut," she said. She proceeded to do so despite Slade's protests, ignored, that it was not worth bothering with.

"And now how about a snack?" she suggested. "I don't know how about you, but I'm famished."

"The best thing you've said," Calder applauded. She headed for the kitchen. "See Amado and Palmer are gabbing again," the sheriff remarked. "Seem to find a lot to talk about."

"Yes, they do," Slade replied thoughtfully.

While they were putting away the snack, Estevan glided in and accepted a drink. Dolores at once showered him with praise, in Spanish, greatly to his embarrassment. He repeated one of his favorite remarks. "To serve *El Halcón* is the honor great."

Eldon Palmer said goodnight to Amado and departed. Slade's thoughtful gaze followed him to the door. And so did Estevan's.

Amado, looking meditative, strolled over and sat down. He gestured toward the swinging doors to introduce the subject of his remark. "He thinks on the side north of the river he will soon the place open. Quite pleased seems he.

"And, *Capitán,* in you the interest he

does take. Asked how come *El Halcón* you are called. I told him that the *peons* of the river villages thus named you because of the big black hawk of the mountains you them remind, that can give, as *Señor* Sheriff would say, an eagle his comeuppance."

Slade laughed. "I've never been quite sure as to whether or not to be flattered," he said.

"Flattery it is not, but of truth the word," Amado said soberly.

"But the mountain hawk is not exactly a dependable critter," Slade pointed out. "He's a roamer, a feathered chuckline rider who is always mavericking off somewhere, never staying for long in one place."

"Exactly," Dolores said pointedly. Slade grinned, forebore getting into an argument and shifted the subject back to Eldon Palmer.

"And what did he say when you told him what you did, Amado?"

The poetic Mexican hesitated a moment, then replied, "Capitán, I

144

had added that to all who sorrow, know oppression or wrong, *El Halcón* is a holy house. *Capitán*, he glanced at you and said that which I did not understand — 'The Dark Ferrash strikes, and prepares for another Guest.' What is the Dark Ferrash, *Capitán*?"

"Death," Slade said quietly.

At the table was a sudden silence.

Finally, Dolores observed, "That remark of his had a familiar ring."

"Slightly misquoted from the Fitz-Gerald rendering of *The Rubaiyat of Omar Khayyám*," Slade explained. "Would seem the gentleman has a smattering of the classics."

"Just the same, I don't like him," Dolores declared.

"Less now than before. What he said sounded disparaging, and — even threatening."

"I had something of the same notion," put in the sheriff.

"But why?" asked Amado.

Dolores shrugged expressive shoulders. "Envy, perhaps, or jealousy; he's the

145

sort that would batten on both."

"He who of Death speaks invites Death's hand," said Estevan, slim fingers toying with the haft of his blade.

Slade was silent, but his eyes were thoughtful.

"Oh, good gosh!" the sheriff suddenly exclaimed. "What with one thing and another, I plumb forgot. Tomorrow is payday for the spreads, the railroads and the dock workers. The boys will whoop it up tomorrow night."

"And because of which I'm going to change right now and call it a night," Dolores said. "Everybody in favor?"

Everybody was.

11

PAYDAY dawned auspiciously, with golden sunshine, a sky of deepest blue and a gentle breeze blowing up from the south. It appeared the cantankerous and unpredictable weather gods had agreed to cooperate.

"Rained last payday, which sorta slowed things up," the sheriff remarked to Slade. "Make up for it today and tonight. I've sworn in three specials, good men I can trust, to help keep an eye on things. Think our outlaw bunch might try to make something of it?"

"Not beyond the realm of possibility," Slade replied. "And could provide us with opportunity, which we badly need. Right now I'm at my wits end trying to figure where the devils will strike next."

"You ain't been doing so bad,"

the sheriff consoled. "Was a real nice collection of carcasses laid out there on the floor, with another one the other side of the river that Estevan did for. And half-a-dozen or so with sliced-up hides to remember you by. Estevan said those four in that Javelina rumhole looked like they'd been run through a meat grinder. Not at all bad, I'd say. But you still haven't any notion who's the head of the pack?"

"I'm getting a vague notion," Slade replied. "Seems so preposterous I wouldn't even mention it yet."

"Well, if you've got a notion, I'll bet a hatful of *pesos* it points a finger at the right sidewinder," said Calder.

"Don't be too sure," *El Halcón* cautioned. "Remember, I had a vague sort of notion about Taylor Ross, and it didn't work out."

"I'm still ready to bet," grunted the sheriff. "Suppose we amble over to the Blue Bell for a while and watch Fats Boyer get rich."

Slade was agreeable, and they set

148

out. Calder glowered at the crowd already packing the streets.

"Going to be a heller, sure as blazes," he growled. "Young hellions, and some not so young, that should know better but don't already rolling in. The paycar in the railroad yards is doing business, and the dock workers have been paid off."

"And the shops and the bars are all set to reap the golden harvest," Slade remarked. "Well, the boys work hard and have a right to a little fun now and then, even the older ones — present company excepted, of course, although you'll have to admit that you enjoy it, too."

The sheriff snorted but did not dispute the allegation, and there was a gleam in his frosty old eyes.

The Blue Bell was crowded, but Boyer had their table reserved for them. They made themselves comfortable — Slade with coffee, the sheriff with a snort of redeye — and looked things over.

Slade spoke. "Something I keep wondering about," he said. "What was the meaning of that gathering in the Casa Mata the night Estevan killed the fellow who was trying to slip up the stairs behind me, and broke it up. There have been such meetings there before, of course — I 'attended' one, at the head of the stairs — that were held by 'liberators', but this time there has been no talk of a liberator, not a word. Both Amado and Estevan are positive of that. The meeting was undoubtedly for something else, and it strikes me as being a bit ominous. What *did* somebody have in mind?"

"Chances are we'll learn soon enough, and it will be something unpleasant," Calder predicted.

Slade thought he was very likely right, but it didn't help much. With a shrug, he dismissed the matter for the time being and gave his attention to his surroundings. He quickly decided that the sheriff was also right in his prediction that it was going to be a wild night; Brownsville was already beginning to howl, and it was still quite early. Before another day dawned, the howl would become a raucous, possibly sinister, screech.

At the moment, however, all was gay hilarity and good fellowship. Song, or what was intended for it, was carolled lustily; the air quivered to whirling words. Glasses hammered the mahogany; bottle necks clinked merrily on rims; the till bell played a blithe tune. Fats Boyer rubbed his hands together and beamed.

"Look at him!" snorted the sheriff. "Every time that bell rings, he grins. What's he going to do with all his money? Never seems to spend much, though I have to admit he gives away a lot. He's an easy touch for anybody who's down on his luck."

"Which, I'd say, is very, very much to his credit," Slade replied. "There are worse vices than generosity."

"Oh, I suppose so," said Calder. "But I hate to see him taken in by some worthless work dodger who never figures to pay him back. Fact is, the squirrel-brain never asks for payment."

"Perhaps the satisfaction that comes from doing a good deed he considers payment enough," Slade suggested.

"You should know where that's concerned," said the sheriff. "You're bad as he is."

Slade laughed and shifted to another topic. "All this is entertaining, but it doesn't help much to solve our problem," he remarked, "Just where will those devils strike? That's the big question which is confronting us."

"So many places they can make a try for," said Calder. "There's the railroad paycar for one. That car will be packing plenty of *dinero* after it finishes paying off here. Come morning, and it will head west for Laredo, Sanderson, Alpine and pay off there. But the railroad police will be guarding the car all night, so I guess that's out."

"Unless that shrewd bunch happens to pull something unexpected and plumb out of the ordinary," Slade answered. "Seems preposterous to even think so, but I still wouldn't put it past them. I think later on I'll have a look at the railroad yards, just in case."

"Not a bad notion," agreed the sheriff. "Best not to pass up any bets, even though they do sound *loco*. I'll go along."

"Not until well past nightfall," Slade decided. "First we'll mosey around a bit and look things over. No hurry; we'll eat first."

Sunset blazed in the west; the dusk sifted down. The street lamps glowed sickly yellow, but silvered as the darkness deepened. Slade and the sheriff gave their orders for dinner.

Deputy Webley and one of the specials dropped in to report no serious trouble so far.

"But I betcha something will cut loose before morning, the way the boys are getting ossified," Webley predicted. "Yes, we'll have a snort, then back on patrol."

Now the Blue Bell was really booming. Slade felt his pulses quicken. It was an old story to *El Halcón*, payday in a border town, but it had never lost its appeal. The unleashing of raw passion has a perhaps reprehensible allure, and he had long since conceded the indisputable fact that the extreme of immorality is as fascinating as the extreme of virtue — and often more so.

So he gazed on the colorful scene with something very near to pleasurable anticipation, wondering just which way the cat would jump next and recognizing that the activities of the metaphorical feline were beyond accurate prediction

"Well, back to the treadmill, trying to figure where those hellions may cut loose," said the sheriff, shoving aside his empty plate. "No stages tonight that I know of. One from Los Indios isn't due until tomorrow; the one from Alice day after tomorrow. Of course the rumholes will all be loaded, but the owners take extra precaution on paydays, so I figure it's unlikely they might make a try for one of them. A little chore of cow stealing might be in the offing, but that could happen any place up and down the river."

"And we can hardly dictate where a widelooping shall take place," Slade remarked. "Looks like we'll just have to sit tight and await developments."

"Figure on crossing the river tonight?" Calder asked.

"Possibly, if Estevan doesn't show up with something," Slade replied. "There'll be a backwash of payday in Matamoros, for a lot of the younger cowhands and railroaders go over there. They find the dance floor *señoritas* to their liking."

"They would!" snorted the crusty bachelor on the other side of the table. "Women! Wherever they are, there's trouble."

"Nice trouble," Slade smiled. The answer he got was another snort.

An hour passed, with the turmoil steadily increasing. Slade glanced at the clock.

"Suppose we walk about a bit," he suggested.

"A good notion," agreed Calder. "Be nice to breathe air instead of smoke for a change."

Although the streets were just as boisterous as inside the bars, the air was considerably better, cool and bracing, with just enough wind to stir the dust under the hoofs of cowhand horses that were arriving from the more distant spreads.

"Getting a late start, and they'll make it a late finish," said the sheriff, nodding toward the new arrivals. "Be noon tomorrow before things really quiet down."

There was plenty of noise and excitement, but no indications, so far as they could see, of serious trouble developing. Gradually they worked their way to the river, without noting anything of more than passing interest. All the places were doing a good business and were, comparatively speaking, orderly.

They paused at the Last Chance and chatted for a while with Sturm and Teresa, who had nothing of importance to tell them. Outside, the sheriff suggested, "How about ambling over to La Luz and seeing what's there? Doesn't 'pear to be anything worthwhile here."

"Might as well," Slade agreed. So they headed across the bridge to Matamoros.

Which was a mistake.

12

AT the railroad yards all was peaceful, with very little activity, for only a skeleton force of those who could not be spared was on duty. The majority of the railroaders were helping celebrate payday.

The paycar stood on a spur close to the street that paralleled the yards on the east. It was a quiet, poorly lighted street with but a few belated pedestrians moving about. There was a light burning in the car, for the paymaster was working on his books. A couple of railroad policemen lounged near the car, keeping a close watch on everything that went on in the vicinity.

There was a sound of hoofs, and down the street rode a half-dozen horsemen. They were almost opposite the paycar when around the corner bulged six more horsemen, going in the opposite direction.

The first group jerked their horses to halt. Another instant and the second group drew rein as abruptly. There was a volley of yells and curses, then a roar of gunfire.

Back and forth gushed the orange flashes, accompanied by more yells. A corpse-and-cartridge session for fair! The few pedestrians dodged into doorways or hit the ground to get out of line with the flying lead.

The two railroad policemen, exclaiming, hurried forward toward the bellowing gunfight — it sure sounded like one. They failed to see the two figures glide from the shadows behind them. Two crashing blows on skulls, and they were stretched senseless on the ground. The gunwielders whirled and raced to the paycar door, where a third man, tall, broad of shoulder, joined them. They dashed up the steps and into the car.

The paymaster, just rising from his chair to see what all the shooting was about, caught a glimpse of three masked figures looming over him. Then he, too, was pistolwhipped to sprawl unconscious.

In a corner, a big old iron safe stood open. While his two companions, guns in hand, stood by the door, the tall man glided to the safe and in a matter of seconds had its money contents, a very large sum, transferred to a canvas sack. Then all three robbers slipped out the door and faded into the darkness. The whole affair had not taken three minutes.

In the street, the shooting stopped. The group from the north whirled their horses and streaked back the way they had come. The second bunch pounded after them.

Men stood up, came from doorways, exclaiming, wondering. Despite all the lead that had been thrown, there was not a single body on the ground. Nor had any of the retreating horsemen appeared wounded.

Not until yardmen hurrying to the

scene stumbled over the unconscious police and discovered the equally unconscious paymaster did anybody have an inkling of what it was all about. Then, however, what it was all about was glaringly apparent, the rifled safe bearing mute witness. And then there was a considerable to-do. "Send for the doctor! Send for the sheriff! Notify the general yardmaster!"

The news of what happened spread quickly, and soon there was a dense crowd about the paycar, constantly augmented by new arrivals.

★ ★ ★

Slade and the sheriff were on the crest of the bridge, returning from their brief visit to Matamoros, when the shooting started.

"What in blazes!" exclaimed Calder. "Sounds like the Battle of Palmito Hill all over again!"

"It's up by the railroad yards," Slade said, quickening his pace. "Tom, I'm afraid we slipped and have had one nicely put over on us."

"You mean the paycar?"

"Exactly," Slade replied. "I'm willing to wager that when we get there we'll find it has been cleaned."

As they hurried down the ramp, the sheriff cocked his head in an attitude of listening. "Shooting's stopped," he said.

"Yes," Slade answered. "They've accomplished whatever they set out to do by it. I only hope nobody was killed. Somehow I've a notion nobody was; that shooting sounded phony to me. We'll learn when we get there, and just what happened."

Naturally they did, some little time later, when they arrived on the scene.

"A novel method to attract attention from the car," Slade remarked. "Worked beautifully. Somebody has brains a-plenty and knows how to use them."

The doctor was already at work on the injured. "I'm afraid the short policeman has a fracture," he told

Slade. "The other and the paymaster ain't hurt too bad. I'll have them packed to my place. You can talk with them later, if you wish to."

A man drew Slade and the sheriff aside. "Something I figure you ought to know," he said. "I got a purty good look at a couple of those devils. They wore cowhand clothes like the others and were all muffled up in their neckerchiefs with their hats pulled down low, but I'm plumb sure they were Mexicans."

"Could be," growled Calder. "Not all the rapscallions are on this side of the river. Much obliged for telling us."

Somebody called the informant, and he hurried away. Calder turned to the Ranger.

"And what do you think of that?" he asked.

"I think," Slade said slowly, "that I'm beginning to get a notion as to the meaning of that gathering in the Casa Mata. I'm pretty sure there were just about a dozen there that night. Yes, somebody is well supplied with brains. We'll discuss it more fully later. Well, I guess there is nothing more we can do here, so suppose we head for the Blue Bell. I don't know how about you, but I'm hungry."

"I'm lank as a gutted snowbird," Calder declared. "Let's go!"

Not unnaturally, when they reached the Blue Bell they found the robbery the chief topic of conversation there. Slade chuckled as he heard a big yardman say, "But it could have been worse. Suppose it had happened last night? Then the chances are we wouldn't have got paid today."

The very thought of such a prospect evoked a dismal groan from his companions.

"And they'll telegraph ahead to Laredo and Sanderson and have more money waiting for 'em, so the boys there won't lose out, either."

"And the roads, using the one car, will share the loss," remarked the sheriff. "Reckon they can stand it."

Slade felt very probably they could as he sat down and gave his order to a waiter.

"You said you were going to have something to say about those horned toads who staged the phony gunfight," the sheriff reminded.

"Yes, I have," Slade replied. "Somehow, the head of the bunch has managed to inveigle some young Mexicans into joining him to perform certain chores like the one tonight. What he has promised them I don't know, yet. Of course there is a certain discontent south of the Rio Grande. For instance, Mexican dock workers over there are paid less for the same work than the Texans on this side of the stream. And unfortunately some of the employers are Texans taking advantage of cheaper labor and providing a fertile field for anybody sowing the seeds of discontent. The people over there feel that they are being imposed upon, which they are.

Beginning to understand?"

"Yes, I am," growled Calder, "and we've got to do something to bust it up or we are liable to have real trouble on our hands."

"And what to do, at the moment, I'm hanged if I know," Slade said. "I'll try and think of something, and I'm going to set Estevan and his boys to work on that angle; they have influence with the younger men."

"And you still don't know who's the he-wolf of the pack?" Calder asked.

"I'm at least beginning to get a fair notion," Slade said grimly. "Although his move was quite successful tonight, I'd say the gentleman slipped a little and tipped his hand, making clear certain things that up to the present had been but a vague and disquieting impression that something was not as it should be where a certain individual was concerned."

"And you're not ready to call names yet?"

"I prefer to try and collect a little

166

more corroborative evidence first," was the Ranger's reply. Calder nodded and did not press for more.

Deputy Gus and one of the specials appeared to report the town unexpectedly quiet with no serious trouble anywhere.

"Interesting how the robbery put a damper on the payday enthusiasm," Slade commented. "Appears to have had a sobering effect."

"Took the young hellions' minds off the gals and the likker for a while," said the sheriff. "Some good coming out of it."

"Good usually comes from evil, sooner or later," Slade observed.

"Like giving you a better line on the head devil of the bunch," Calder remarked shrewdly.

"Exactly," Slade agreed.

The hours passed, and the crowd began to thin out. The babble of words died to a murmur. The faro dealer levelled off his chips. The card dealers dropped their decks into the drawers. Weary bartenders poured final drinks as Boyer sounded his last call. Soon the Blue Bell would be dark and silent, save for the kitchen, where the cook and his helpers were still busy.

The east flushed rose and gold and liquid saffron. A little breeze shook down myriad dew gems from the grass heads. Birds began their morning song, homage to the king of day.

Estevan and Dolores Malone entered.

"I thought with her the bridge across it was best to ride," the knife man explained.

"You were right," Slade told him. "We'll have a talk this afternoon. How was La Luz?"

"We were very, very busy, but no trouble," Dolores replied. "I was on the floor most of the time, and gracious! I am tired."

"And you're calling it a night right now," Slade said.

They walked her horse to the stable through the golden glow of the dawn.

13

IT was late afternoon when Slade and the sheriff sat in the office and discussed the situation.

"Maybe after making that big haul last night the devil will lay off for a while," Calder suggested.

"I doubt it," Slade replied. "I have a feeling he is obsessed by a compelling urge for constant action. Quite probably, too, with a money lust. I'm of the opinion he will be constantly on the move whenever he sees something that will promise excitement and gain."

"I suppose so," the sheriff agreed wearily. "Blazes! But it's hot. Going to be a change in the weather; I'll bet on that. Storm building up, or I'm a heap mistook."

"Feels that way, all right," Slade answered. "Well, I'm heading across the bridge for a word with Estevan. Meet you at the Blue Bell for dinner."

He walked out into the brassy sunshine. On the crest of the bridge he paused and gazed southwest, where a cloud was rising, an ominous purple cloud that rolled, fold on fold, from the horizon.

It was one of the Rio Grande country's yellow days, one sort which around Sumatra or Borneo would presage a typhoon. Slade could feel a tingling in his blood, an acceleration of his pulses. He knew, of course, that there were electrical charges about, which accounted for the eerie symptoms. But this prosaic explanation couldn't quite banish a premonition of evil to come. He shrugged his shoulders and walked on, eyeing that ominous cloud which was rising higher and higher.

Reaching La Luz, he found Estevan awaiting him. He gave the knife man some precise instructions.

"Keep an eye on him as much as you can, and if he leaves town, try and learn where he's headed for," he concluded.

"That, *Capitán*, I will do," Estevan promised. "Of that one, I for the some time have been suspicious." He drifted out.

Dolores and Amado were at work in the back room, and at this hour business was slack. Slade grew increasingly restless. Finally he took to the streets.

No great distance to the southwest from town was a hill. Obeying a sudden impulse, Slade made his way to the hill and climbed the slope to the crest, from where he would have a better view of the coming storm. For now there was no doubt but that a real storm was building up. Lightning flickered over the breast of the cloud, which had passed the zenith; there was a mutter of distant thunder; and the wind was rising.

On rolled the cloud, until there was but a narrow streak of blue autumn sky above the northern horizon. At the south base of the slope was heavy growth, and from it came a rustling sound, as if a giant were stirring there, gently pressing the leaves back with his great hands. Louder, more insistent — the giant was growing impatient. A breath of moving air, another, harder, fanned Slade's face. And came the wind, a roaring, bellowing wind, and with it a torrent of icy rain.

Overhead the sky was rent by jagged flames of lightning. The boom of the thunder shook the hill. Harder blew the wind. The air was dark almost as night, save for the intermittent glare of the lightning, in the blaze of which the rain became long threads of scintillating fire.

The sky was asunder. Blue flame crackled in the air. Following a thunderclap that seemed to rock the universe, with a louder howl of the wind, came a veritable waterfall of rain. Slade was beaten to his knees. Another moment and he stretched out flat on the ground. He was not given to nervous tremors, but it *was* an exposed and elevated spot, a fit target for the thunderbolts; wise to make himself as inconspicuous as possible.

Abruptly the rain lessened, the wind lost some of its force, objects became visible, and Slade saw he was not alone. Standing not twenty yards away was a tall and broad man he instantly recognized as Eldon Palmer, gazing to the south.

Through the blanket of cloud, flowing from a hole in the overcast that looked like an eye, came a red ray from the setting sun, which fell where Palmer was standing. Had he been the center of the stage scene, no spotlight could have set him off to better advantage. His clothes were 'garments rolled in blood.' His face was rapt, flooded with an unearthly ecstacy. He flung out his arms in a wild, abandoned gesture.

As if by command, the eye in the heavens shut, and the ray went out. Blackness seemed to flow in from every quarter. The lightning blazed anew and fell earthward in a flame spout of fire; the thunder crashed; the rain came down in a flood that rendered all things invisible. Slade lay motionless, waiting for a cessation in the war of the elements.

It came, almost at once. The wind hushed; the rain ceased to fall. In its place a garment of completest calm descended upon the earth, with only little soft sounds, as if the trees were weeping silently together. The sun, low in the west, reappeared. And Slade realized that he was alone on the hill crest. Eldon Palmer had vanished, as if gone with the wind, the thunders and the rain.

Rising to his feet, Slade walked slowly down the slope and to town. He was drenched, wet to the skin, and cold, but he took no thought to physical discomfort, hardly acknowledged its existence. For now he understood the truth: his opponent was a madman. One glance at his face in the red light from the eye in the sky had convinced

Slade of that. Yes, Eldon Palmer was a madman, with a madman's ruthlessness and cunning.

Despite its really commonplace nature, the experience had given birth to an eerie feeling where Eldon Palmer was concerned. Out of the storm he had come; into the storm he had gone, like some stark elemental harnessing the tempest to its own dark ends. Slade laughed at the fantasy and turned his thoughts to more mundane things.

Foremost was to get the hell across the river and into dry clothes, for the night air was growing chill, and there was a limit to what even his iron constitution could resist. He proceeded to do so.

He chuckled to himself as he changed clothes. Eldon Palmer was really insane, drawing a behaviour parallel, what was to be said of his own sanity? He, too had walked to the hill crest to face the storm. He chuckled again as he recalled what the old Quaker said to his friend: 'Everybody is mad save thee and me, and I sometimes have my doubts about thee!'

When he reached the Blue Bell, Slade found the sheriff awaiting him.

"Looks like you were under cover when the storm cut loose," Calder observed.

"I wasn't," Slade replied.

"No? Where the devil were you?"

Slade told him, exactly, including his conclusions anent Eldon Palmer. The sheriff showed few signs of emotion.

"So that's the hellion you figure to be the head of the pack, eh? I've been getting a notion to that effect for a while; you've been paying a lot of attention to him."

"Yes, he's the leader of the outfit," Slade answered. "And I fear he is going to take considerable handling."

"And what we going to do about him?" Calder wanted to know.

"A very nice question," Slade replied. "Suppose you come up with the answer."

"Oh, you'll come up with it, all right;

no doubt in my mind as to that; just a matter of time," the sheriff declared confidently. "Let's eat."

They did, and felt the better for it. For a while they sat silent with coffee, a snort and smokes. Then the sheriff asked, "Just how did you come to tie up Palmer with the outlaw bunch?"

"It just sort of worked itself out," Slade replied. "First, the rather vague descriptions given by people who happened to witness the bunch in action tied up with Palmer's physical appearance. Then there was his definite interest in me. Not much to go on, but it did cause me to take a mild interest in *him*. And he was always around just before or just after an attempt against me was made. All of which could mean little or mean a good deal. Of course, as I mentioned, the real tip-off came when he had his young Mexican dupes stage that sham gun fight to draw attention from the paycar. I had already learned he had quite a bit of influence with the younger Mexican element, especially the *vaqueros* and dock workers. Right then I knew very well the meaning of that mysterious meeting in the Casa Mata; it was to discuss what Palmer had planned and what part he wished them to play.

"He's been telling them that they have a right to be revenged against those they believed have wronged them, especially those on this side of the river, and has promised to get them better pay and better working conditions if they will string along with him. Old stuff, but it works, especially with the ignorant. I have Estevan and his boys working to counteract that angle by telling them that *El Halcón* says Palmer is not the friend they think he is and will do nothing but lead them into trouble."

"And what *El Halcón* says is believed," the sheriff commented. "Anything else?"

"Not much," Slade admitted. "Only the paymaster got a glimpse of the three who knocked him out and mentioned that one was tall and broad shouldered, Palmer's description again. So there's my case against him, which wouldn't be worth a darn in court, as you very well know."

"He'll get the decision against him in Judge Colt's court," said Calder.

"Very likely," Slade conceded. "I doubt if he'll ever be taken alive. Well, we'll see."

"And in the meantime you are on a nice hot spot," said the sheriff. "The devil will sure be after you."

"Perhaps, and perhaps it will be for the best," Slade returned carelessly. "May bring him out into the open."

Calder snorted and addressed himself to his drink. "Now what?" he asked.

"I think I'll amble across the river to La Luz and see if Estevan has managed to learn anything," Slade decided.

"And I'm amblin' right along with you," the sheriff declared with decision.

"Always nice to have pleasant company," Slade accepted, and they set out.

Crossing the bridge without misadventure, they reached La Luz, where they found Estevan awaiting them, a perturbed Estevan.

"*Capitán*," he said without preamble, "him I to follow tried, but I lost him in the rain."

"Never mind," Slade answered, "I found him."

"*Si*? And where, *Capitán*?"

"On top of that hill to the south of town," Slade replied.

Estevan shook his head. "Assuredly he is *loco*," he declared. "None but one who is *loco* would have been on the top of that hill during the terrible storm."

"I've been wondering about that myself," Slade grinned.

"And how does *Capitán* know he was there?"

"Because I saw him. Because I was there, too."

"*Nombre de Dios*!" swore Estevan, staring.

"Yes, he's *loco*, all right," Slade said.

"And I'm beginning to think I may be in the same category."

"*Capitán* the joke makes," replied Estevan. "Him in his *cantina* I left. I return to see if there he remained." He glided out, and Dolores occupied his chair. She looked Slade up and down.

"Would appear you stayed under cover during the storm," she commented.

"Don't you think I have sense enough to come in out of the rain?" *El Halcón* countered.

"Knowing you as I do, I'm not at all sure," she retorted. "I want a glass of wine."

The wine was quickly forthcoming, and Slade, recalling the slight chill he had experienced, had one with her. The sheriff settled for redeye.

The time jogged along. Dolores changed to a street dress. Amado prepared to sound his last call. Estevan slipped in, looking despondent; evidently he had failed to kill anybody.

"That one in his *cantina* the night

remained," he reported. "To some young men he talked, not so many as before, for to some my *amigos* had already talked."

Slade stifled a grin; Estevan's *amigos* had a 'striking' way of emphasizing their remarks which the wise did not lightly disregard.

"You're doing all right," Slade told him. "And so are your *amigos*; they are a big help."

"The better I soon to do hope," Estevan promised. He finished a drink, bowed to *El Halcón* and departed. The others also called it a night.

14

SHERIFF Tom Calder and Ranger Walt Slade were both beset by a feeling of frustration as again in the office they discussed matters pertaining to Eldon Palmer and his bunch of outlaws. Where would the devils strike when they did strike? And Slade was convinced they would, and soon.

Item by item, they went over the possibilities and arrived at no satisfactory conclusion. Calder fetched coffee from the back room, hoping from a swig or two they might glean inspiration, especially when it was well spiked from the bottle he had in a drawer. Slade, less hopeful, took his straight. As they sipped and smoked, they again reviewed the tedious chore, and again with negligible results.

"I'm still hoping Estevan will turn

up with something," Slade observed.

As a matter of fact, Estevan did. It was not long after full dark when he entered the office with his peculiar gait, his black eyes snapping, his usually impassive countenance animated. He accepted a chair and coffee, spiked, and spoke.

"*Capitán*," he said, "I know not but it something may mean. I watched the *cantina* of the *ladrón*, Palmer. In were four men I had never seen before, but whose looks I liked not. They talked with Palmer, had drinks. He the back room into went, to return soon wearing the garb of the rangeland. The four men out came and mounted *caballos* tethered the rack at. They waited. Me they saw not, for I was in a doorway dark across from the *cantina*. They talked together, and I one heard say, 'The fifteen miles about west of Progresso.' I heard no more. The *ladrón* Palmer out came and the *caballo* mounted. All rode the bridge across. I too rode the bridge across, to tell *Capitán* what saw I and heard." He paused, expectant.

"About fifteen miles west of Progresso!" snorted the sheriff. "What in blazes? There ain't nothing there." But he, too, looked expectant, fixing his gaze on Slade.

For several minutes Slade sat silent, his black brows knitting.

"Tom," he said, "I'm not so sure there is nothing there. I am familiar with that section. Just about fifteen miles west of Progresso, or a couple miles less, is a little-travelled side trail that runs from the main north-south trail to Hidalgo on the north bank of the Rio Grande. You'll recall we were mixed up in a shindig at Hidalgo about a year and a half ago, when we saved storekeeper Arbuckle's money he had stashed under the floor of his store."

"By gosh! That's right," said Calder. "Saved it from Waldron Lang and his hellions you later cleaned up. You figure something like that might be in the wind?"

"I don't know," Slade admitted. "I hardly think it would be anything paralleling that."

"*Capitán*," Estevan put in eagerly, "much money the river crosses from Hidalgo these days. From Reynosa in *Mejico* the quantities large of fine wines and brandies are brought to Hidalgo, where the buyers wait to pay out *pesos* the great many for the — contraband — I think it called is."

"You're right about that," Slade said. "Smuggled stuff that pays no duty."

Smuggling was viewed with tolerance along the border, viewed as a legitimate activity so long as you didn't get caught. The Rangers gave it little attention.

But of late Slade had heard rumors of a syndicate being formed to make smuggling big business in defiance of federal and Texas law. Another example of the new type of criminal invading the West, bringing big city methods to bear. Sooner or later this would mean real trouble with rival factions gunning for each other and the outlaws

186

endeavoring to cut in on the fat profits. Law-enforcement officers, including the Rangers, would be forced to take notice and act. And the sooner the better.

"Our *muchacho* may have hit on something," Slade told the sheriff. "I've a feeling it will bear a little investigating. And there sure doesn't seem to be anything else lined up. When you can think of nothing, give heed to somebody who can think of something. Round up the deputies, and let's take a little ride. Guess they have close to an hour's start on us, eh, Estevan?"

"*Si*, the hour and a little less," the knife man replied.

"I don't think they'll push their horses much, seeing as they have quite a jaunt ahead of them, and we should be able to close in on them when they reach Hidalgo, if that's where they're headed for," Slade said.

"And I've a prime notion that's where they are headed for," said Calder. "This may be our big chance." He hustled out to round up the deputies, which didn't take long, because he knew where to find them. At the stable they cinched up with speed, while Estevan waited on his rangy mustang. Ten minutes later found them riding west on the river trail.

Past Santa Rita, La Paloma, Los Indios, and Santa Maria they rode at only a moderate speed, the hour being early and people still moving about, and Slade not wishing to attract attention. He preferred to give the impression of a bunch of cowhands heading for home after a day in town.

However, after passing Progresso, he quickened the gait and constantly scanned the back trail, although he thought it unlikely they would be followed. But with such a character as Eldon Palmer it was best to take no chances; he was undoubtedly a master of the unexpected with an uncanny ability to anticipate the actions of another.

Soon, though, satisfied they were not wearing a tail, Slade gave his whole attention to the terrain ahead. "Wouldn't put it past him to have a trap set for us somewhere, improbable as that would seem to be," he explained to Calder.

"And we sure don't want to bulge into one," replied the sheriff. "That sidewinder gives me the creeps just to think about him."

"You should have seen him on that hilltop during the storm, with the red ray of sunlight clothing him in blood," Slade chuckled.

"I'm glad I didn't," growled Calder. "Bad enough to hear you tell about it. How much farther would we have to go before we turn off toward the river, do you figure?"

"Less than three miles now," Slade replied, "and it's getting along toward midnight. I've a notion we will close in on Hidalgo at just about the right time, perhaps a bit earlier. The smugglers would hardly begin operating until the town has quieted down for the night with nobody on the streets. So take it easy from now on until we sight the lights of Hidalgo. Then we'll try and figure what is the best move to make."

Finally they reached the side track that wound through stands of chaparral to ultimately slither like a dejected snake down a slope to the little town and the river.

Now Slade's vigilance increased, for if there was a trap somewhere ahead, this was the place to set it. He constantly scanned the brush with eyes that missed nothing, watched carefully for startled birds rising from the thickets to announce that there was something nearby that alarmed them. He breathed relief when they paused at the brink of the slope, screened by brush, and saw below a scattering of lights that was Hidalgo. Only a few hundred yards distant flowed the turgid flood of the Rio Grande, silvered by the glitter of stars.

"This is as far as we can risk," he whispered. "No telling just where the devils are, if they're there at all. We'll just have to wait and see what happens. I prefer to stay in the saddle, for we may have to move fast if something breaks. Remember, Tom, when we saved Arbuckle's money from Waldron Lang and his bunch, they set fire to an old barn across the river in Reynosa to attract everybody from the vicinity of his store. I don't think Palmer will resort to anything that crude. Whatever he does will be original and unexpected. The devil only knows what, so we must be on the lookout for anything. All right, take it easy; it's up to them to make the first move."

"And here's hoping we make the last one," Calder replied in as near a growl as a whisper could attain.

The wait that followed was long and tedious, without even the solace of a smoke to break the monotony. But gradually the lights of Hidalgo winked out until the little settlement was dark and silent.

Slade constantly scanned the river and the far bank, where the lights of Reynosa still twinkled. It was beginning to look like they were following a cold trail, but his hunch insisted otherwise.

Abruptly he leaned forward in the saddle. Near the far bank movement had birthed. It resolved into a big flat-bottomed scow being poled across the river by two boatmen; beside them were other vaguely revealed forms.

"Get set!" he breathed. "We should have action any minute now; the smugglers are on their way from Reynosa."

Another moment and shadowy forms materialized on the north bank; the buyers were preparing to receive the contraband.

The scow, the star-silvered water rippling away from its sides, beached. There followed a bustle of activity, and then activity of another and most unexpected form. Slade's keen ears caught a thud of beating hoofs. Another instant and five horsemen bulged into view from the west, shooting as they came.

Yells, curses, screams of agony echoed the reports.

"My God!" gasped the sheriff. "They're shootin' 'em down like sheep!"

"Come on!" Slade shouted. "Shoot fast! It's snake-blooded murder!"

He sent Shadow racing down the slope and swerved to the right, the others pounding behind him, firing as fast as they could pull trigger.

"Up!" Slade roared. "You are under arrest! In the name of the State of Texas!" He shot with both hands even as he spoke.

A saddle was emptied, and another. Caught utterly by surprise, the outlaws, nevertheless fought back viciously. Slugs whined past the posse. One ripped through the crown of Slade's much-abused hat. Another shredded his shirt sleeve. He fired again, and a third owlhoot fell. The posse's guns blazed in unison, and only one rider, tall, broad-shouldered, a mask hiding his features, remained erect in the hull. He whirled his horse, a big bay, and sent it dashing straight for the scow. The bay took the rail like a bird and landed on the bottom of the scow with a crashing of hoofs, his rider whipping from the saddle.

There was a shot, a yelp of pain, a voice bawling orders. The terrified boatmen shoved the scow away from the bank, the current caught it, and it went scudding downstream. Slade tried to line sights with the outlaw but could not distinguish him from the other occupants of the scow and was forced to hold his fire. The posse also stopped shooting, but all set to blaze away again could they catch a glimpse of the target.

"No use," Slade told them. "He's gone, the he-wolf of the pack."

The scow was now but a smudge on the water. Slade gazed after it, gave vent to a disgusted oath. So darn close, but the devil made good his escape. He gave attention to his immediate surroundings

Three of the buyers were dead, two more painfully but not too seriously wounded, Slade concluded. One was unscathed.

Now lights were flaring up in the nearby houses, heads poking cautiously outdoors. Slade turned to the uninjured buyer.

"You know folks here, don't you?" he asked.

"That's right," the buyer admitted.

"Okay," Slade said, "tell them to fetch lights so I can take care of these men who are hurt."

The buyer hurried off to care for the chore. Soon lanterns were forthcoming, with people trailing after them, mostly silent.

With Estevan lending a deft hand, Slade secured his medicaments from his saddle pouches and went to work on the wounded. soon he had the wounds smeared with antiseptic ointment, padded and bandaged, the bleeding checked.

"That should hold them for the time being," he said. "Some of you folks put them to bed and give them hot coffee, plenty of it. I'll have the doctor ride out from Brownsville tomorrow and look them over."

"We'll take care of them, Deputy," said an elderly, capable-looking individual. "And would you like for me to bring you boys a pot of coffee?"

"Best thing you've said yet," Slade accepted. "And please send word to Sheriff Dave Judson of Hidalgo County of what happened. Tell him we're taking the bodies of the outlaws to Brownsville to put them on exhibition, that he can come and claim them if he wishes to do so, which is unlikely."

The outlaws' horses, docile beasts, had remained close by. The bodies of the owlhoots were draped across their saddles while the men waited for the coffee. Slade wondered how many of the smugglers aboard the scow had been murdered. No way to tell. The two boatmen, if Palmer didn't kill

196

them also, wouldn't do any talking after putting him ashore somewhere down the river, very likely on the Mexican side, from where he would make his way back to Matamoros via the Camino Real, completely in the clear again.

Calder went through the pockets of the dead outlaws and unearthed quite a bit of money. He pocketed some, winked at Estevan and shoved the remainder in his hand.

"Guess he and his *amigos* have earned a mite of celebration," he said to Slade.

"They have," the Ranger agreed. "Were it not for Estevan, we wouldn't have been here tonight with the opportunity of doing a good chore, even though the big fish did slide out of the net."

The boiler of coffee arrived, along with it a stack of tasty sandwiches, to which the posse did full justice.

Before setting out, Slade made a few pointed remarks for the benefit of the uninjured buyer, a rather young fellow, and received some frank answers.

"Nobody pays much mind to smuggling along the river, but you had an example tonight of what it can lead to," Slade concluded. "Think it over the next time you get the notion to go for easy money that is liable to turn out very *hard* money."

"Deputy," the other replied, "I'm through with this business for good and all. I'm going right back to followin' a cow's tail."

Slade believed him.

"Well," the Ranger observed as they climbed the slope, "Well, we didn't do so bad. Gor rid of some scum the earth can well do without, saved the buyers's money and kept Palmer from making another really good haul. And, I believe, we reformed one smuggler. I gathered from the young fellow I talked with that he inherited a small spread, sold it and began investing the proceeds in the smuggling business. The lure of easy money, the 'golden calf,' is still held aloft. But where he's concerned, what happened tonight somewhat tarnished the image."

"All of which, so far as I can follow you, means we did a pretty good chore, everything taken into consideration," said the sheriff.

"Precisely," Slade agreed. "We didn't bat a hundred, but our average wasn't too bad."

"Your average is a good deal more than a hundred anybody else was able to do before you showed up," grunted Calder.

Unscrambling that one, Slade smiled and let the apparent percentage discrepancy pass.

"I can't get over the way that hellion managed to slip through our fingers," the sheriff grumbled. "Did the last thing I would have expected him to do."

"His brain functions like a well-oiled machine," Slade commented. "He instantly realized what was his one chance to escape and took advantage of it. Everything he did was perfect. As soon as he landed in the boat he was out of the saddle and shooting one of the smugglers to impress the boatmen, which it did. They didn't argue with him an instant. He was crouched among the other occupants of the scow, and I had to hold my fire for fear of hitting one of them. Oh, he's a shrewd one, all right; don't know as I ever contacted a smarter. Nor one more callously disregardful of the sanctity of human life. The buyers never had a chance. No warning, just lead poured into them."

"And if you hadn't figured things so we caught the devils off balance, the chances are we would have been mowed down, too," declared Calder.

"The element of surprise was in our favor," Slade conceded.

It was long past daybreak when the weary posse reached Brownsville, and they created excitement a-plenty as they made their way to the sheriff's office, where the bodies were laid out on the floor.

"Come around later and look 'em over," Calder told the crowd. "Right now we crave shuteye."

The horses were cared for, and the posse, one and all, went to bed, not to rouse up till late in the afternoon.

15

SLADE and the sheriff ate at the Blue Bell, then opened the office to the curious. The results were the same as with the other bodies. Several citizens were pretty sure they had seen the outlaws hanging around the various bars, but that was all.

To the comments Slade paid scant attention. He knew who was his man, especially seeing that Estevan at once recognized the dead raiders as the four men in whose company Palmer left his *cantina*.

"So all we have against him is association with criminals," *El Halcón* remarked to the sheriff later. "And that would be a very fragile stick to lean on in the court of law; a good lawyer would with little difficulty break the stick. Nobody got a look at his features, for he was masked when the buyers were attacked. Nobody recognized him as Palmer, and I certainly couldn't swear that the man I saw ride his horse into the scow was Palmer, no matter how convinced in my own mind that it was. In other words, he is still in the clear, and we have nothing against him."

"Guess that's right," Calder agreed. "But wouldn't you say he is getting sorta short of hired hands?"

"It would look that way," Slade replied. "And there's no doubt but he's losing his hold on the young Mexicans; Estevan and his *amigos* are taking care of that, which helps. But he can get more followers if he wants them. Up till recently he had been doing very well, and a leader who can show results doesn't have much trouble drawing that element to him, especially in this section."

"It's crawlin' with 'em," growled the sheriff. "So it all sums up to we've got to get the sidewinder dead to rights."

"Definitely," Slade said. "And, viewed

by past performance, it looks like a hefty chore."

"I've noticed you sorta thrive on hefty chores," Calder said cheerfully. "Don't figure this one to be an exception. By the way, Doc jogged up the Hidalgo to have a look at the patients. He'll be back tomorrow to hold an inquest.

"Maybe we can round up a couple more specimens for him to work over," he added hopefully.

"I fear you are unduly optimistic," Slade smiled.

"Maybe, but how about moseying over to La Luz? Amado might have something to tell us."

"A good idea," Slade agreed. "I'd be going over there later, anyhow."

The sheriff locked up, and they set out, crossing the bridge without incident. Matamoros was bustling; La Luz, busy and gay. Slade noted at once that there was an unusual number of young *vaqueros* and dock workers present. They bowed and smiled and waved greetings.

"Looks like Estevan and his boys are getting in their licks," he chuckled to Calder as Amado escorted them to their table. "Those are quite a bunch of the young fellows who used to hang out in Palmer's *cantina*, or I'm greatly mistaken. Which is all to the good; at least we won't have to worry about something cutting loose over here or a raid by those young hellions on the Texas shore."

"Just mentioned *El Halcón*, the chances are," grunted Calder. "That's all they had to do. Plenty of influence."

"Thanks for the compliment," Slade returned smilingly, "but Estevan and his boys also pack a mite of *influence* of their own; it is quite persuasive!"

Amado filled glasses. Dolores waved from the dance floor. A few minutes later, Estevan appeared.

"Not the day nor the night long has the *ladrón* in the *cantina* been seen," he announced.

"Maybe he fell in the river and got

drowned," hoped the sheriff.

"Highly unlikely," Slade differed, "but I've a notion his prolonged absence may well mean trouble in the making."

"Yes?"

"Yes. I'm just wondering if he has a hangout someplace where others of the bunch he did not deem necessary to take along in the raid against the buyers were awaiting him. If so, I'm playing a hunch that he will strike again soon, and I haven't the slightest idea where. Got any suggestions?"

"Not a darned one," growled Calder. "But I have got a prime feeling that you're right." Slade laughed and turned his attention to Dolores, who came bouncing over from the dance floor.

"I'm going to keep Estevan right beside me all night, so he won't be able to lead you into trouble," she stated with emphasis.

"Fates worse there could be," replied Estevan, his teeth flashing white in his dark face.

"A penchant for paying nice compliments is a catching thing, like fever or the sleeping sickness," said Dolores. "It exudes around Walt; no man can come within five paces of him without catching a spark."

"Guess the same thing can be said of flattery," the sheriff observed pointedly. "Present company excepted, of course."

"See!" gurgled Dolores. "He's caught on, too."

Big old Dave Judson, Sheriff of Hidalgo County, rolled in and shook hands all around.

"Fats Boyer told me you were over here, so I thought I'd drop in for a gabfest," he said. "I read the riot act to those three buyers who are still able to navigate. They seemed sorta subdued."

"I imagine what happened to the other three had a somewhat sobering effect," Slade commented.

"If it didn't, nothing will," declared Judson. "You sure did a fine chore,

Walt. A pity one of the owlhoots made it in the clear."

"Yes, it is," Slade agreed.

"I feel pretty darn sure it's the same bunch that has been running off cows over to the west, in Starr County," Judson pursued. "Sure have been smart the way they've handled it. I figure it to be one of the worst outfits we've ever had operating here, and that's saying plenty." Again *El Halcón* was in agreement.

They chatted together for quite a while. Slade and Dolores danced several numbers. Judson, a good story teller with an unusual fund of dry humor, kept his companions chuckling, Estevan drifted out, returned shortly and shook his head. Slade's black brows drew together. More and more he was convinced that Palmer had something in mind. Well, if it was set for tonight, there was nothing he could do about it; very likely it had taken place already. If so, they'd hear, and doubtless not enjoy the hearing.

Time jogged along. The sheriffs began yawning. Estevan gave up watching the *cantina* and went to bed. Dolores changed to a street costume and glanced suggestively at Slade. The stars smiled down benignly as they crossed the bridge and walked the deserted streets.

★ ★ ★

Early the following afternoon, Slade and the sheriff had a visitor. Taylor Ross, the grape farmer, dropped in. He shook hands heartily with Slade.

"Heard about it, what happened at Hidalgo," he said. "A fine piece of work, Mr. Slade, very fine. Must have given the hellious something of a jolt. Just had to come and congratulate you."

"Thank you, Mr. Ross," Slade answered. "Could have been better, but I guess it could have been worse. Have some coffee with us; perhaps you'll like yours spiked, as the sheriff takes his."

Ross accepted and for some moments sat silent. Abruptly he said, "I did wish to congratulate you, Mr. Slade, but that wasn't exactly what I came for. I saw something that somehow I felt might interest you. I'm an early riser, you know, and I was up this morning well before daybreak. I walked over to my west arbor just as it was getting a bit light. Heard horses and saw six fellers riding west on the trail. But after they passed my fenced holding they all of a sudden turned north. They didn't see me because I was in the shadow of the arbor, but I could see them very well. I watched them ride on and on, veering a bit to the east, until they were out of sight. Couldn't help but wonder why they were riding that way. No ranches up there and no farms. Nothing but open prairie for miles. You know that west of my holding for a couple of miles there are no farms, not till you are but a few miles from Progreso. What do you think?"

"I think," Slade replied slowly, "that

you may have hit on something of interest, all right. Unless I'm mistaken, less than a mile west of your place is a very good ford, a ledge that runs from the north to the south bank of the river, with heavy brush growing along the banks."

He turned to Calder. "Remember, Tom, Dave Judson mentioned last night that there has been quite a bit of widelooping over in western Hidalgo County and Starr County. That caused me to do a little thinking at the time, and what Mr. Ross has just told us sort of ties in with it. As he says, to the north is nothing but open brush — prairie, with hills farther on. Nothing, it would seem, to attract a bunch of dawn riders. Unless they happen to have a hole-up where they can lie low during the daylight hours and have figured a way to run off a herd of beefs by way of the ford west of Mr. Ross's holding."

"By gosh! That sounds plumb reasonable," agreed the sheriff.

"So, all in all," Slade summed up, "I think we'll take another little ride west tonight."

"Say!" exclaimed Ross. "Can't I go with you? I'm a pretty good shot, and I could stand a mite of excitement; growing grapes gets a bit monotonous."

"Glad to have you," Slade replied. "Estevan will want to go along too; I'm expecting him to drop in any time now."

"Doc McChesney will hold his inquest on those carcasses over there on the floor in an hour or so," said Calder. "But that won't interfere.

"With the deputies and Mr. Ross and Estevan we'll count up to five," he added. "Six you saw, I believe you said, Ross, so the odds won't be too lopsided. That is, if Walt has it figured right and they do plan to run off a herd, from maybe Tol Grundy's holding. Oh, he's right, no doubt as to that. Playin' one of his blasted hunches, bless 'em!"

"Yes, I'm willing to wager that what

Mr. Ross saw was Palmer and the rest of his bunch and that they mean business," Slade said. "By the way, I think you should deputize Mr. Ross to make it regular."

"Right again," agreed the sheriff. "Hold up your right hand, Ross."

The grape farmer did so. Calder mumbled a few words, and it was done. Ross was staring at the Ranger.

"Mr. Slade, do you mean Eldon Palmer is the leader of the outlaw bunch?" he asked incredulously.

"He is," Slade stated flatly.

Ross whistled between his teeth. "Eldon Palmer!" he repeated. "I'd never have suspected it."

"Nor wouldn't nobody else but Slade," grunted Calder. "Oh, the sidewinder is smart, all right, but not smart enough to fool *El Halcón*."

Ross shook his head in wordless admiration.

Estevan strolled in, accepted a cup of coffee, spiked, slanted his eyes toward Ross and glanced questioningly at Slade, who nodded. "Not the day has the *ladrón* in his *cantina* been," he announced.

"And that also ties up," Slade observed.

Shortly, Doc McChesney and his coroner's jury arrived, and a brief inquest was held, the verdict being justified homicide by law-enforcement officers in pursuance of their duty. Court adjourned.

"Now all we can do is take it easy and wait for night," Slade decided. "We won't leave town until after dark. I figure they won't be likely to operate before midnight, which gives us plenty of time to reach the ford, get under cover and be all set for them to show."

"And 'fore long we'll eat dinner at the Blue Bell," said Calder. "Getting ready to bust up an outlaw bunch always makes me hungry."

His suggestion was followed, and they enjoyed a leisurely meal. The deputies, Webley and Gus, had been notified to meet them at Agosto's stable, and shortly after full dark they again rode west past the familiar towns.

"Gettin' so I know every crook and turn of this blasted snake track," Calder growled.

"A little luck tonight, and it may be the last time you'll ride it for a while," Slade told him.

16

FOR a while Slade scanned the back trail. But he was fairly convinced that none of Palmer's followers were hanging about town and that the chance of them being tailed was negligible. Not long after they passed Santa Rita, he faced to the front and quickened the pace.

His companions chattered gaily as they rode, but Slade was mostly silent. It looked like just a routine chore that could be handled without too much difficulty, but he had a wholesome respect for Eldon Palmer's shrewdness. It almost appeared at times that the cunning devil was gifted with the second sight and could foretell the future. Ridiculous, of course, but past performance had rendered the absurd presumption almost plausible.

They passed Ross's cabin, in which

a low light burned.

"When I ride to town alone, I always have one of my boys spend the night in the shack, just in case something might happen," he explained.

They covered the best part of another mile. Slade slowed the pace and began studying landmarks.

"About three hundred yards more and we reach the ford," he told the others. "There's a track leads down the slope to it, flanked on each side by chaparral. Just west of the track, where the growth is heaviest, we'll make our stand."

A little later he drew rein. "This should do it," he said. "Now we'll take it easy and await developments. I'll see and hear them coming along before they will be able to sight us. Then we'll hole up beside the track and, if things go right, bag the whole bunch."

"Sure sounds plumb perfect," said Calder.

"Yes, *sounds* that way," Slade agreed.

"Well, we'll see."

He was not as confident as were his companions, for he was experiencing an uneasy presentiment that all was not as it should be. Why he should feel that way he hadn't the slightest idea, but he did.

The wait was a long one. An hour passed with nothing happening, and the best part of another. Then suddenly Slade leaned forward in the saddle. His keen ears had caught a sound which he instantly recognized as, faint with distance, the peevish bawl of a weary steer.

Again came the sound, not yet audible to the others, and Slade uttered a disgusted exclamation.

For the sound had come *not* from the north, from where he had expected it to come, but from the east by slightly north.

"What's the matter?" Calder asked.

"Outsmarted again, that's what," Slade replied bitterly. "The devils aren't heading the cows to this ford, as we figured they would, but to the one well east of Mr. Ross's holding. Come on! I think we should still be able to get there before they are across the river. If we can just catch them out on the water, the advantage will be ours."

His voice rang out: "Trail, Shadow, trail!"

The great black lunged forward and in seconds was going at top speed, steadily distancing the other cayuses, who were pounding along behind him, giving their best, which wasn't enough.

Slade knew it was foolhardy to draw away from the rest of the posse, but he was in a mood to risk anything. And if he could just close the distance enough to get his highpower Winchester into play, he'd be able to account for one or two of the devils no matter what the final outcome would be.

They flashed past Ross's farm, and he saw the cows. They were streaming down the high, heavily brush-grown bank to the water. Behind them were six riders, urging them on. Slade drew the big rifle from the saddle boot and cocked it but shook his head; the distance was still too great for anything like accurate shooting in the very poor light.

"But they'll never get the critters across the river in time," he exultantly told Shadow. "And if they stop and try to shoot it out with us, they'll be tangled up with the cows and we'll still hold the advantage. Easy, feller, easy; let the other boys catch up."

Shadow leveled off to a smooth running walk that hardly jolted his rider. Slade estimated the distance, raised the Winchester. Six hundred yards, maybe a little more. Now the six riders were almost to the growth. He clamped the rifle to his shoulder, glanced along the sights and squeezed the trigger.

The report rang out like thunder. He saw a rider lurch sideways in his saddle but keep his seat. White blurs that were faces turned in his direction. There was an answering flash; the slug struck his left stirrup iron. The shock threw him off balance as he squeezed the trigger a second time and scored a miss. Before he could recover, the last of the riders had vanished down the slope.

"But we've got them trapped, feller," he said as the posse pounded in behind him, shouting and swearing. Together they raced ahead, guns out and ready for business.

A sudden glow! A flicker! A tongue of flame that licked upward through the tinder-dry brush! Almost instantly the whole dense stand was a roaring inferno, with clouds of smoke billowing up to hide the river and everything else.

Too thoroughly disgusted to even swear, Slade reined in, the others jostling to a halt beside him and making up for his lack of vocal expression.

"The blankety-blank-blanks!" bawled Calder. "Who ever heard tell of the like!"

Slade had regained his composure.

His sense of humor came to the rescue, and he chuckled; there was really something comical in the old sheriff's rage. His own chief reaction was one of utter admiration for Eldon Palmer's resourcefulness.

"Take it easy 'fore you bust a cinch," he advised Calder. "We're outsmarted, and there's nothing we can do about it."

Meanwhile he sat with his rifle ready against the faint chance the fire might burn down and the smoke cloud lift enough to reveal the wideloopers while they were still on the water.

Finally it did lift enough to show the six horsemen vanishing into the growth that clothed the distant south bank of the river. He emptied the Winchester's magazine in their general direction, more to relieve his ruffled feelings than anything else, for he had little hope of scoring a hit. The posse followed his example and banged away cheerfully until the cartridges gave out.

"Hold it!" Slade called. "We've

wasted enough powder for one night."

"The blankety-blank-blank!" the sheriff raved again. Estevan did even better, for he could swear in three languages. The efforts of Ross and the deputies were feeble by comparison.

"We cuss and he giggles!" growled Calder. "Walt, do you think the hellion knew we were waiting for him at the other ford?"

"I wouldn't put it past him," Slade replied. "He appears able to figure everything in advance." He gazed at the smoldering brush fire that was fast burning itself out for lack of fuel and gathered up the reins. "Guess we might as well mosey to town," he said. "Maybe better luck next time."

"Stop off at my shack first for coffee and a bite," Ross suggested.

"A darn good notion," said the sheriff. "I've done cussed myself empty."

Ross's young Mexican, who had been aroused by the fire and the shooting, met them at the door with a cocked sawed-off shotgun for company. He bowed to *El Halcón*, wanted to know what it was all about.

Estevan, speaking Spanish, explained matters. The youth regretted he hadn't been there to share the fun and hurried to the kitchen.

Some time later, fortified by the coffee and the snack, the disgruntled posse set out for Brownsville, arriving at the river town shortly after daybreak.

"I just can't get over what happened tonight," Calder complained as they stabled their horses.

"Yes, it was unique," Slade said. "Either evinced the most careful planning in advance against all possibilities, with meticulous attention to details, or that hair-trigger brain of his instantly sized up the situation as it stood and reacted accordingly, arriving at the only decision that would serve his ends. As I told you, he's something to go up against."

"My money's still on *El Halcón*," answered the sheriff. "Let's go to bed."

17

AROUND the middle of the afternoon, as they discussed the previous night's happenings, the sheriff asked, "Whose cows were those the devils tied onto, would you say?"

"I'd say they were some of Dixon Lanham's Bar L critters, the chances are," Slade replied. "His spread is the farthest west."

"Well, if so, he won't feel the loss overmuch," said Calder. "He's pretty well heeled after you finagled that deal for him with the irrigation people when you were here last and they paid him a whoppin' big price for a hunk of his land. But he won't like it."

Slade's guess turned out to be accurate. An hour or so later, a gentleman in a bad temper showed up. It was Dixon Lanham, the Bar L owner.

"Nigh onto a hundred prime beef stock run off night before last," he announced. "How they managed to slide them past my patrols to the south and reach the river is beyond me. I can stand the loss, all right, but it riles me to have a thing like that put over on me. How they did it I'm hanged if I know, but they did."

"Yes, they did," Slade agreed. Briefly, he recounted the happenings of the night before.

"When did you discover the loss?" he concluded.

"Late yesterday afternoon," Lanham answered. "Yes, those must have been my critters, but how in blazes did they do it?"

"I'd say that the members of the bunch who didn't take part in the raid on the smugglers night before last widelooped the cows, ran them into the hills and held them there during the daylight hours, then circled them around to the west under cover of darkness and slid them down to the crossing west of your land," Slade replied.

"Which means the devils have a hangout somewhere to the north, eh?" the sheriff put in.

"At least a hole-up for the cows," Slade said. "Two raids in one night! The gentleman is ambitious, all right. An old trick, running the cows into the hills that way, but handled skillfully, it works. And you can depend on our *amigo* handling anything skillfully."

"I thought you ought to hear about it, although I figured there was nothing you could do, getting the word so late," Lanham observed.

"Glad you told us," Slade replied. "And incidentally, it might be a good idea to patrol your north holding some, as well as to the south."

"You've got something there," Lanham agreed. "I'll do it from now on."

After Lanham had departed to the Blue Bell in search of liquid refreshment, promising to meet them there later,

Slade remarked to Calder, "Cattlemen and cowhands are, as a rule, creatures of habit. Do a thing a certain way, and they keep on doing it that way until they get a jolt that alters their viewpoint. Had Lanham patrolled some to the north, he would have saved his stock."

"Uh-huh, they're good on hindsight but poor when it comes to foresight," the sheriff answered. "Think what he told us might be a help?"

"It could be," Slade said. "At least we now know just how it was done, although I had a fairly good notion anyhow."

"Imagine you did," grunted Calder. "You don't miss many bets."

"I missed one last night," Slade countered smilingly.

"And who the blinkin' blue blazes could have figured that one in advance, I'd like to know," snorted the sheriff. "I'll fetch us some coffee. Feel the need of a swig, well spiked, every time I think of it."

When they entered the Blue Bell a little past sunset, Slade feared for an instant that Calder really would bust a cinch, for standing at the bar, debonair, impeccably groomed, was Eldon Palmer. He waved a greeting, which the sheriff managed to return.

"Careful," Slade warned. "If he doesn't know we suspect him, keep him that way."

"The blankety-blank's laughin' at us," Calder muttered.

"Well, after last night I guess he has a laugh coming," Slade said.

"He'll laugh on the other side of his face at the finish," the wrathful peace officer predicted.

Although he knew what the sheriff meant, Slade had a feeling that Eldon Palmer *would* laugh at death even as he laughed at life.

Dixon Lanham was also at the bar but at once joined them and insisted on buying a drink. And, much to Slade's amusement, Eldon Palmer sent a round over from the bar before strolling gracefully out. The outraged sheriff surreptitiously emptied his onto the sawdust. The outlaw leader, Slade concluded, had a Machiavellian sense of humor.

"Juanita sent regards," Lanham remarked. "Said she hoped to see you before you left the section again."

"I hope so, too," Slade replied. "Tell her hello for me, and I expect I'll drop over at your place during the next few days."

Juanita was Lanham's wife, a little red-haired beauty, a former La Luz dance-floor girl. Slade and Dolores Malone had been instrumental in getting them together.

They finished their dinner, and after a snort of redeye to hold it down, the sheriff suggested, "Suppose we cross over to Matamoros for a while?"

"An idea," Slade agreed. "Estevan may have something to tell us; he will have been circulating all evening."

"And I'd like to have a little gabfest

with Amado and the boys," added Lanham.

"When they reached La Luz, without incident, Dolores was on the floor; Amado, at the far end of the bar, where Lanham joined him. Slade and Calder occupied their usual table.

Slade was silent and distraught. The sheriff watched him, puffing his pipe but offering no comment. He knew *El Halcón* was pursuing something up and down the corridors of his mind, and he had learned to respect those silences.

Slade was indeed pondering a move. Finally he arrived at a decision, dismissed the matter for the time being and relaxed comfortably.

Estevan drifted in, appearing to be in a bad mood. "The *ladrón* at his *cantina* is," he announced. "He looks the — what do you call it — smug."

"Doubtless he feels smug, after the good haul he made last night," Slade pointed out. Estevan said something in Yaqui that Slade felt would not bear translating.

"My blade it thirsts," Estevan added, caressing the haft of his knife.

"But remember, we still have nothing on him," Slade cautioned. "Keep it in its sheath until the time is ripe to use it." Estevan grunted, downed a drink and glided out to do a little more scouting around.

Dolores joined them, and she and Slade danced several numbers. But business was slack, and Slade and the sheriff were still a bit weary after the hectic happenings of the night before, with not much rest. Dolores swore she scarcely had slept a wink before going to work. Lanham had decided to spend the next day in town and not return to his spread until late in the evening. Estevan dropped in again with nothing to report. So everybody called it an early night.

★ ★ ★

A couple of hours past full dark the following evening, Walt Slade again rode west on the river trail. He paid little attention to the back track after passing Santa Rita, for he thought it highly unlikely that he had been followed out of town. And if he had been, he was amply prepared to take care of any tail that might endeavor to affix itself to him.

He rode steadily west until he passed Taylor Ross's dark cabin and grape arbor, then turned north, veering somewhat to the east until he knew he was passing across Lanham's land. The miles flowed back. From time to time he sighted clumps of cattle, fine, heavily fleshed beasts, grazing or lying down around waterholes.

But as he continued north, these became less frequent, for the grass was thinning and parched by the sun. He reached a last waterhole no great distance from the beginning of the brush grown slopes, the ridges and the washes. Stars dimpled its surface, and it was evidently spring fed. He passed it and rode on until he reached the slopes. Spotting a wash that looked promising, he turned in it and followed it to where a trickle of water from a spring formed a little pool around which grass grew.

Stripping off the rig, he turned Shadow loose to graze. Then he spread his blanket and with his saddle for a pillow was soon fast asleep.

The morning chorus of the birds awakened him some time before dawn. He sluiced his head and face in the cold waters of the pool, then kindled a tiny fire with dry wood, confident the faint trickle of smoke would not be noted by any chance watcher, the presence of one being highly unlikely.

As usual, there were cooking utensils and staple provisions packed in his saddle pouches along with a helping of oats for Shadow. Soon coffee was bubbling in a little flat bucket; bacon and eggs, sizzling in a small skillet. The addition of a hunch of bread made a satisfactory breakfast for a hungry man.

After eating, he again stretched out

and smoked in full-fed comfort until the first rays of the sun gilded the hilltops. He cleaned up and packed the utensils, cinched up and started his quest, his objective the spot where the widelooped cattle had been corralled, possibly the outlaws' hangout.

There were old cabins in the brush country, built by trappers and hunters of long ago. He visited several in the course of his search but discovered no indications of recent tenancy.

All day long he rode the slopes, the ridge and the washes and discovered — nothing! He knew there was a limit to how far from the river the herd could be held, and he had already passed that limit. Finally, with the sun almost to the western horizon, thoroughly exasperated and quite a bit puzzled, he turned back to the open prairie, reaching it not far from the big waterhole he had noted the night before.

"Guess you can stand a swig of that," he told Shadow and sent him moseying toward the pool.

Suddenly he leaned forward in the saddle, staring. There were no cows around the pool or anywhere in sight, but there was ample evidence that a large number of cows had been here recently and for quite some time, a full day at least.

And *El Halcón* understood!

★ ★ ★

"The nerve of that sidewinder!" he said to Shadow. "Rounded up the critters farther south during the night, ran them here and held them in close herd all day, *in plain sight*! Then when darkness fell, drove them south to the river ford, where he set fire to the brush after we spotted them. This is utterly ridiculous!"

But after gazing around for a few moments, he realized it was not as ridiculous as appeared on the surface. In every direction, one could see across the prairie for miles. No chance rider could approach to investigate the herd without being spotted by the rustlers. Nearby was a straggle of brush that would effectively conceal them. Very unlikely anybody would ride this far north. Very fortunate nobody did. That would have meant a killing, for Eldon Palmer didn't go in for half measures.

Yes, if some of Dixon Lanham's Bar L hands had ridden this way, he would now be just that many short.

And once again, Palmer had shown example of his astounding resourcefulness and his uncanny ability to recognize any opportunity, no matter how ephemeral, that might present itself.

Rolling a cigarette, Slade sat wondering were it possible to make capital of his discovery, reluctantly concluding it unlikely.

"Lanham will be patrolling to the north tonight as well as by the waterfront," he explained to the horse. "The bunch would find it much more difficult to round up a herd, and the chances are they'll next turn to something they consider easier. What? I haven't the slightest idea. Appears to be a chronic condition with me of late — low man on a guessing pole. Let's go home!"

Shadow, having slaked his thirst, was willing, and they set out through the gold and scarlet of the sunset that littered branch and twig and flooded the grassheads with molten fire.

He and his horse both tired after a long and hard day, he let Shadow choose his own gait, and it was well past midnight when they reached Brownsville. He cared for his weary horse, made sure all his wants were provided for and made his way to the Blue Bell, where he found the sheriff awaiting him and looking expectant.

While waiting for a meal to be prepared, Slade recounted his experiences. "The hellion is the limit," he concluded. "And he always seems a jump ahead of me."

"He wasn't ahead of you when he

tried to wreck the Port Isabel train and when he tried to rob the smugglers," Calder reminded. "Didn't have any luck trying to drygulch you a few times. I'd say the score is about even."

"Under the circumstances, just being even isn't good enough," *El Halcón* replied morosely. "The unpleasant fact remains that he's still on the loose, which means more trouble."

"He'll be the one to corral the real trouble before all is finished," the sheriff predicted confidently.

"Hope you're right," Slade replied. "But I still maintain I've never gone up against his equal; he's positively uncanny."

"Here comes the chuck," said Calder. "Let us eat!"

They proceeded, taking their time about it, and they had just finished and were enjoying their after-dinner smokes when Estevan and Dolores Malone arrived.

"Knowing you had ridden off some-where and would be tired when you got back and would stop here first, I had Estevan escort me across the bridge," the girl said.

"Thanks for being so considerate," Slade answered. "I'll admit I am a bit weary."

"A good night's sleep will take care of that," replied Dolores.

"That's right, a good night's *sleep*!" remarked the sheriff. Dolores ignored him.

"The *ladrón* in his *cantina* has the night been," said Estevan. "There I think he will stay."

"Very likely," Slade agreed. "Forget him for the time being; we'll take him up again tomorrow."

18

THEY did take him up — with a vengeance — late the following afternoon, for Estevan's *amigos* reported he had not been seen in the *cantina* all day.

"Which means he's up to something, sure as shooting," Slade declared.

"But what?" wondered the sheriff.

"A nice question, with, so far, no answer," Slade replied.

It was Dixon Lanham, dropping in unexpectedly, who provided, indirectly, what Slade believed was a possible answer, giving him a clue to work on.

"Had to come to town to put in an order for some needed supplies," Lanham explained. "Thought I'd drop over and tell you I'm patrolling to the north, too, as you suggested."

"A good notion," Slade agreed and gave the rancher an account of what he had discovered in the course of his ride to that section of the Bar L range, much to Lanham's astonishment.

"What a bunch!" he exclaimed, adding a few adjectives that wouldn't look well in print.

"Business is going to pick up here tomorrow," he continued. "I stopped at the irrigation project for a gab with Clark. Tomorrow is payday there, and Clark is providing his boys with transportation to Brownsville so they can have a regular payday bust. Hundreds of 'em, well heeled, and they're good spenders. Yes, business had ought to pick up. Think maybe I'll stay over to take part in it."

Slade stared at him, glanced at the clock, then abruptly rose to his feet.

"See you in a little while," he told his surprised companions and hurried out. He made his way to the Brownsville bank, arriving there just before closing time. He had no difficulty obtaining an audience with the president, an old friend.

"Clint," he said without preamble after they shook hands, "Clint, did Ernest Clark tie onto his payroll money today?"

"Why, yes, Walt," the banker replied. "Quite a hefty chunk, too."

"And took it to the project head-quarters, of course."

"Don't know what else he'd do with it," said the president. "Something in the works, Walt?"

"Clint, I don't know for sure," the Ranger answered. "There could be. Thanks for what you told me; I'll be seeing you again soon."

As he watched *El Halcón's* tall form pass out the door, the president remarked to his ink stand, "I think some sinner is due to catch it!"

Slade did not return to the office at once. He wished to do some hard thinking without interruption and, if possible, to evolve a plan. Standing near the river, watching the sunset, he envisioned the irrigation project, which he knew was progressing with speed. Clark was running his laterals and leads. Before long he would be ready to tap the river water and fill the ditches and the impounding basin, for the workers were giving their best to the popular engineer. They deserved a day of relaxation and diversion.

And it was such men as Eldon Palmer who clogged the wheels of progress for their own selfish ends. Well, he'd see about that in this particular instance, at least. He headed for the office.

When he arrived there, he found the sheriff alone, Lanham having departed to attend to his business matters.

"Well, have you got the answer?" Calder asked.

"I presume to believe I have," Slade replied.

"Yes?"

"Yes. I dropped in at the bank, and Clint, the president, told me Clark packed his payroll money to the project today. It will be in his office safe tonight, of course, and I doubt it will be adequately guarded. Clark is a good man, but he's an engineer, not a law-enforcement officer. Besides, he can't think of everything."

"Different from some I can mention," said the sheriff. "Do you figure the devils might make a try for that money?"

"I think it probable," Slade answered. "It would make a nice haul. And I certainly can't think of anything else. So, if you are agreeable, tonight we'll take another little ride."

"You're darn right," Calder instantly agreed. "I believe you've hit it, and this may be our big chance."

"That's the way I see it," Slade said. "Anyhow, I figure we have everything to gain and nothing to lose."

"What time shall we leave?" asked the sheriff.

"About an hour after dark," Slade decided. "That will give us plenty of time to get there. By then the camp will have quieted down. Unlikely the hellions will attempt anything until well past midnight. Locate the deputies and line them up. I'm expecting Estevan here at any minute. If he reports Palmer still among the missing, I feel sure it will mean we're riding a hot trail. We'll eat at the Blue Bell and be all set to go."

Estevan arrived shortly, shaking his head after a fruitless watch over Palmer's *cantina*. He was acquainted with what was planned, looked pleased and fingered the haft of his knife.

They ate a leisurely dinner, repaired to the stable, where the deputies awaited them, cinched up and once more rode west under the stars. They passed Santa Maria, and before reaching the spot where the trail dipped down to the river, Slade turned north.

"We'll circle the project and approach Clark's office building from the north," he said. "It lies a little distance from the temporary barracks where the workers sleep and was built to be permanent and remain in use after the project is finished, to house those who oversee the workings. Just to the north of it is a stand of brush that will come in handy, perhaps."

Now Slade quickened the pace and constantly scanned the star-burned prairie in every direction with eyes that missed nothing, for he certainly did not desire a head-on collision with the outlaw bunch seeking the same objective, the office building.

With a sense of relief, he finally sighted the two-story structure looming against the sky. The bristle of thicket but a little distance to the north would provide concealment for the horses, did they reach it without mishap.

It was a ticklish proposition approaching the growth in the light of the stars, uncomfortably bright. If the outlaws had already arrived and were holed up in its shadow, the results would be highly unsatisfactory from the posse's viewpoint.

However, luck was with them, which isn't always the case where the virtuous are concerned. Five more minutes and they were swathed in its comforting gloom.

"I figure that, if they are headed this way, they'll approach more to the west, farther from the barracks," Slade said. "Anyway, we'll risk it."

He dismounted and dropped the split reins to the ground, all that was needed to keep Shadow right where he was until called for. The others tethered their mounts securely to trunks or branches. They grouped together and discussed the situation.

"There's a back door to the shack which very likely will not be locked," Slade said. "Usually no reason to lock up here. I think our best bet is to hole up inside the building. Then if they do attempt something, we'll be in a position to catch them dead to rights."

"Sounds reasonable," Calder agreed.

"All set?" Slade asked. "Let's go!" At a swift pace he led the way across the open to the door.

As he had anticipated, it was not

locked. Turning the knob gently, he opened it a crack and stood listening, hoping that Clark had not posted a guard inside the building who would shoot first and ask questions later. However, he felt sure if one was inside, his ears would detect his presence, by his breathing if nothing else.

The building remained silent as a tomb. Slade opened the door, gestured the others to enter and, locating a key in the lock, turned it. Now nobody could enter by way of that door without kicking up some racket.

It was logical to believe that the robbers, were there some on the way, would enter by the front door, the office being in the front of the building and to the right.

Enough starlight filtered in to enable *El Halcón* to vaguely distinguish objects. He moved forward, slowly and carefully, paused.

"Here's the stair to the second floor," he told the others. "I'd say back of it will be our best bet — can see into the office from here."

In accordance with his directions, the posse took position.

Light filtered into the office through two windows, and as their eyes adjusted to the gloom, they could make out large objects, chiefly a table-desk and a big iron safe directly opposite one of the windows.

"Don't see how in blazes the sidewinder can slip out of the loop this time," Calder muttered. "But, blast it! The light's getting bad."

It was true. Cloud rack was drifting across the skies, dimming the starlight. Soon they could no longer see the desk and the safe. Slade wondered uneasily if even the elements were going to react in Palmer's favor.

But starlight or no starlight, sheltered as they were by the stairs, they should be able to command the situation. Yes, the set-up was perfect.

And then, disquietingly, there drifted through his mind the blasphemous remark Napoleon, confident in his advantageous position, was supposed to have made on the eve of the Battle of Waterloo: '*Not even God Almighty can deliver Wellington from my hand now*!'

And then that night it rained! Just a brisk summer shower. Just a few drops of water. But as a result, Napoleon's artillery, on which he depended, was bogged down and could not move until the soaked ground had dried, and the battle that was supposed to have started at six o'clock in the morning did not start until ten, giving Blücher ample time to come to Wellington's rescue and turn the tide of battle, and with it the destiny of the world.

A rather far-fetched parallel, yes, but blast it! Where Eldon Palmer's nefarious activities were concerned, it applied. He could very likely be depended upon to provide the 'drops of water' that would further his ends.

The tedious minutes dragged by, and Slade began to have doubts, surely if something were planned it was overdue taking place.

And then abruptly he tensed. To his ears had come a whisper of boots on the heavy grass outside.

"Get set!" he breathed to the posse. "They're coming."

The sound ceased, and another took place, a faint rattling and clicking. The front door opened, letting in a draft of cool air. Slade drew both Colts, cocked them. Again the whisper of cautious footsteps.

A dark lantern was turned on, its beam centering on the face of the safe. By the reflected glow were dimly revealed six masked men moving toward the safe, one tall and broad. Perfect!

And then Eldon Palmer got his break!

19

SOMEBODY had left a scantling leaning against the stair rail. Deputy Webley, seeking to steady himself, reached for the railing. His hand brushed the scantling, and it fell with a rattling crash.

A chorus of startled exclamations. The lantern beam snapped off. A streak of fire, the crack of a gun. A bullet fanned Slade's face.

"Shoot!" he roared and squeezed both triggers. He heard a thud as of something falling.

It was a battle royal in the blackness. The booming of the guns, shouts, screams of pain, curses crackled the shingles of the roof. Boots pounded the floor boards; the front door slammed open. Slade leaped forward, floundered over something on the floor, caromed into the desk. Over it went with a bang. He recovered his balance, rushed out the door. But now the sky was heavily overcast, the darkness intense. He thought he heard a whisper of footsteps somewhere ahead, raced in that direction, heedless of possible consequences.

The beat of feet ceased, was almost instantly replaced by a thudding of fast hoofs fading into the west. Slade halted, wordless; there was really nothing to say.

"Hold it!" he called to the others, who were pounding after them. "Hold it, they're gone."

"But not all of them," the sheriff panted exultantly as he pulled up alongside Slade. "There are carcasses on the floor back there; I fell over one."

"But, I'll guarantee, not Palmer's," the Ranger replied. "Let's go see." They retraced their steps to the office.

The nearby barracks was bumbling like a hive of disturbed bees. Lights flashed up; doors opened; heads thrust cautiously out.

"Come along," Slade shouted. "Everything's under control"

"Anybody hurt?" he asked.

"Nope," said Calder. "That stairway we were under served us mighty well; the devils shot over our heads."

In the office matches were struck, one touched to the wick of a bracket lamp. The glow showed three bodies on the floor. Beside one was a hand drill for boring out the combination knob of the safe. The dark lantern lay nearby.

The masks were stripped off, revealing hard-lined countenances contorted in the agony of death swift and sharp. Nothing outstanding about them, Slade felt. Eldon Palmer was *not* one. And this did not surprise *El Halcón* in the least.

"I knew very well he had escaped again when I heard somebody making for the door," Slade remarked. "Seems like he continually gets the breaks, or makes them."

"Next time I'll bet will be his last,"

the sheriff predicted. "We didn't do so bad. Saved the payroll money and thinned out his bunch a bit more. I'd say it leaves him only two horned toads to traipse along with him."

Now the workers were streaming into the office, exclaiming, questioning. Several remembered Slade from Laredo and greeted him by name. He let the sheriff explain matters, which Calder proceeded to do, evoking admiring glances and comments directed to the Ranger.

Ernest Clark, the engineer, appeared. "So you did it again, eh?" he remarked to *El Halcón*.

"At least we saved your payroll money," Slade smiled.

"Hear that boys?" Clark said. "If it wasn't for Mr. Slade, you wouldn't be having your payday celebration to-morrow."

"Ain't a bit surprised," said a Laredo man. "He's always doing things like that." There was a chorus of agreement.

Calder went through the dead men's pockets, confiscated quite a bit of money and reported nothing else of significance.

"We'll have the bodies carted to town for you tomorrow," Clark told him. "Now come over to the cook shanty for something to eat."

Slade told Webley and Gus to first locate the horses ridden by the dead men and strip off the rigs.

"We'll put 'em in one of the stables," Clark offered. "You'll find them there when wanted.

"I suppose I should have had a guard posted in the office tonight," he remarked as they headed for the cook shanty.

"Very likely fortunate you didn't," Slade said. "It's a killer bunch."

After a bountiful snack and plenty of hot coffee, the posse set out for Brownsville, arriving there after daybreak. The horses were cared for, and everybody went to bed.

When Slade finally roused up, Brownsville was already quite lively, for several hundred brawny irrigation workers were beginning to whoop it up.

Cowhands who could get away from the spreads were also arriving to take part in the fun. And the citizens of Brownsville, not exactly a stodgy lot, could be depended upon to do their share to make the celebration a success.

"Paydays getting to be a regular thing hereabouts," Sheriff Calder chuckled. "Well, the more the better; good for business."

He gestured complacently at the three blanketed forms lying on the floor.

"Clark brought 'em in as he promised he would. Look real purty there. I can't wait till I see the other three in the same shape. Got any notions?"

"Not yet," Slade replied. "I'm still only about half awake, and I haven't had any breakfast."

"Guess Dolores went to work, eh?"

"I suppose she did," Slade replied smilingly.

The sheriff chuckled again. "Then how about ambling over to the Blue Bell for a surrounding?" he suggested. "Can stand a bite myself, and a snort or two to hold it down."

"An idea," Slade agreed. "Then I'll try and do a little thinking, and just possibly I'll hit on something."

"Expect our *amigo* Palmer is in good shape to be hogtied after losing out on a nice fat haul last night," Calder said. "And I've got a notion he is just about at the end of his twine."

"The way things break for him, or he makes them break, I wouldn't want to bet on it," *El Halcón* replied morosely. "He's the limit with bells on." The sheriff didn't look much impressed.

They found the Blue Bell crowded. Slade was greeted by waving hands and shouts of acclaim and was forced to decline offered drinks enough to float a river steamer. He settled for something to eat and coffee.

"Cook's already spotted you, so here we go for more pounds," said Calder. "Eating with you is a calamity; no resisting what he puts out when you're around."

"I think you'll manage to survive," Slade replied, glancing at his lanky form. Once again the sheriff didn't look impressed. However, he did full justice to what was set before him.

"Wonder if Palmer will show up again?" he remarked as he loaded his pipe. "If he does, I betcha he won't look so smug as last time."

Slade was not so sure, for he felt that Eldon Palmer throve on opposition, with an occasional defeat rendering him just that much more resourceful and aggressive.

Ernest Clark dropped in and joined them. "Been circulating around through the various places, gabbin' with my boys," he said. "Wouldn't be surprised if a number of them are over at Matamoros, or will be later on."

"Quite likely," Slade replied. "We'll

be going over there ourselves after a while. To a place I believe you'd like, if you care to join us."

"Be glad to," the engineer accepted. "I feel I can stand a mite of relaxation after last night's excitement. Think I'll go over to the bar, now, for a jabber with the boys there."

"A good man," observed the sheriff. "His boys seem to think a lot of him."

"Yes, they do," Slade agreed. "They know he's for them — first, last, and always. If they have a grievance, they know they can take it to him and be sure of receiving a sympathetic and understanding hearing. The kind of a man who has made and is making this great country of ours what it is despite such scalawags as Palmer."

"You're right there," Calder said soberly. "We could use more like him."

"You'll get them," Slade predicted. "More and more the right sort of people are taking over the Border. But a matter of time until outlawry is a thing of the past.

"And," he added, his eyes dreamy, "later there will be a strong and progressive country south of the Rio Grande that will stand shoulder to shoulder with America in her hour of need. It's coming, Tom. Just be patient; it's coming!"

And regarding his sternly handsome countenance glowing with inspiration, the old law-enforcement officer believed that what he said was gospel truth. He smoked in silence for a few minutes, then: "I think it *would* be a good notion to drop across to Matamoros after a bit."

"Yes," Slade replied. "Estevan may have something to tell us. Chances are he's been very busy."

"After what happened last night, maybe the hellion will lay off for a spell," Calder suggested.

"Were it anyone but Palmer, I'd be inclined to agree," Slade said. "But he's so utterly unpredictable there's no telling how he will react. All we can do is be on our toes all the time and try to anticipate what move he is likely to make."

"You did a pretty good chore of anticipatin' yesterday," the sheriff commented.

"That was sort of made to order," Slade belittled. "It was obvious that the payroll money would be tempting to any outlaw bunch."

"Uh-huh, only nobody else thought of it," said Calder. "But one of your hunches done crawled into my head, and it says we're mighty, mighty close to a showdown."

"Hope it's a straight one," Slade answered. "For I'm growing just a mite weary of the constant suspense."

Just the same, he chuckled inwardly as he said it, for he was honest enough with himself to admit that he really enjoyed pitting his wits against such an opponent as Eldon Palmer. It lent a zest to life that nothing else could quite equal.

Now the Blue Bell was really booming, the bar crowded, nearly every table occupied. The dance floor was jam-packed; the roulette wheels spun merrily, the little balls clicking cheerily from slot to slot. The whoops of the winners blended with the maledictions of those who lost. Cheerful maledictions, however. "Make it next time! Hurrah for Hell! Who's afraid of fire!"

Meanwhile, Slade studied faces, listening to scraps of conversation his keen ears could catch. For the Blue Bell had one thing in common with the Crosby House at Beaumont; sooner or later everybody showed up there. The Blue Bell wasn't crawling with oil millionaires as was the Crosby House, but it was frequented by potential millionaires. For instance, the great Stillman Banking House, one of America's outstanding financial institutions, had its inception in Brownsville.

Also, as in the Crosby House, there were always present gentlemen who would bear watching. So *El Halcón* watched and listened, hoping to hit on something that might prove of value where his personal problems were concerned.

They were the problems, too, of the millionaires-to-be, for that matter. For were not outlawry curbed, it was doubtful they would ever attain the status of Wall Street tycoons.

Yes, in 1877, the Man of Destiny entered Brownsville, unheralded and unsung, and it is unlikely that at that early date he regarded himself as a Man of Destiny.

Just as other men of destiny rode into Brownsville, giving no thought to themselves in such a role. Nor could Walt Slade, that night in the Blue Bell, look down the years to come and vision the tall, broad-shouldered man, a former Texas Ranger, his thick black hair sprinkled with gray, who was the successor to James G. 'Jaggers' Dunn as General Manager of the great C. & P. Railroad System. Verily, one generation passeth away, and another generation cometh!

20

CALDER ordered another snort, Slade, another cup of coffee. They drank slowly, mostly in silence, each busy with his own thoughts.

"Yep, the boys are whoopin' it up," the sheriff finally observed. "Wouldn't be surprised if there are some scuffles before the night is over. But I've got a couple of good specials to lend Gus and Webley a hand, so I guess we can keep things under control. How about tying onto Clark and crossing over to Matamoros?"

"Reckon we might as well; time's getting along," Slade agreed.

The engineer was all set to go, and they made their way through the crowded, boisterous streets and crossed the span without incident to find Matamoros also more than usually lively.

"I like it over here," Clark said. "Folks always seem gay and happy, with too darn many of them having little to be happy about."

"Time will come, and it's not so far off, when they will have more to be happy about," Slade predicted. "Well, here's La Luz. Ever been in this place, Clark?"

"No, I haven't," the engineer replied. "Looks interesting."

"I venture to believe you'll find it so," Slade said.

"Nicely lighted, too," Clark remarked. "Nothing to beat wax candles, plenty of them, for really attractive lighting. So soft and warm."

"Makes the dance floor gals prettier, too," said Calder.

"Oh, they're all pretty, looked at through the bottom of a whiskey glass," Clark chuckled. "Say! I'll take it back; the ones here are all right without a glass. Here comes a little beauty, now."

"Careful," the sheriff warned. "That's

Walt's private property."

"He shows good taste," Clark rejoined. "But I'm not bucking that kind of competition; I'll find me another."

"Let Dolores do the choosing," Calder advised. "She knows how to pick 'em."

After being stopped by several patrons, Dolores finally reached the table. Clark was introduced.

The usually sober and reserved engineer developed an unexpected fund of sprightly small talk, and they got along well together. He turned to *El Halcón*.

"Mind if I ask her to dance, Mr. Slade?" he said diffidently.

"Well, that's what she's here for. She's a dance floor girl, some of the time. But the lady confers, so ask her," Slade replied.

"She confers without a formal request, Mr. Clark," Dolores answered. "Come along."

Clark danced very well, Slade thought. After the number was finished, Dolores beckoned a tall, nicely formed girl with dark brown hair, gray eyes, and sweetly turned lips. She evidently introduced the pair, for they started the next number together. Dolores returned to the table.

"Carmencita will take care of him," she announced. "And now, Walt, perhaps you can spare the time to dance a number with me."

Slade was agreeable, and they had three numbers together, the last a fast one, leaving Dolores bright-eyed and rosy and demanding a glass of wine. Clark and Carmencita were sharing a bottle of wine at another table.

"'Pear to be hitting it off," Calder remarked. "Glad to see it."

"She's all right, a nice girl," Dolores said. "For that matter, you know Uncle Amado won't have any other kind; they've got to play the game square with the patrons. He likes to see them get together, but no taking advantage."

Estevan strolled in, shook his head. "Not the day or the night at his *cantina*

269

has he been seen," he said, accepting a glass of wine.

"Doubt if he will show up there tonight," Slade replied. "It's already quite late."

"Perhaps," conceded Estevan, "but watch more I do." Finishing his wine, he departed.

La Luz was gay and somewhat noisy, but peaceful enough. Elsewhere it was otherwise.

★ ★ ★

The Javelina *cantina*, where Slade had the ruckus with the four outlaws who sought to kill him, was doing a roaring business; for in addition to the regular patrons, quite a number of the irrigation workers appeared to find the place to their taste and were whooping it up for fair.

In the back room, with the bar door locked, the rotund owner was summing up the day and night's take, which was plenty. His eyes gloated greedily over the packets of bills and the rolls of gold coins resting on the table before him.

A fight started between two men at the bar, a hitting, gouging, butting scuffle, all sound and fury. The crowd clustered around them, whooping them on.

In the back room, the owner leaped to his feet, cursing, and started to sweep the money into a drawer. Then abruptly he froze, rigid, staring.

The back door, which was also supposed to be locked, had opened, and into the room stepped a tall masked man, a gun in his hand, which he trained on the shivering owner.

"Sit down, stay down and keep quiet if you want to remain alive," the gun holder ordered. The owner obeyed. The masked man swept the money from the table into a sack he carried, making sure none was left behind. In the barroom, the other side of the locked door, the row was going strong, and noisier than ever. He glanced in that direction, holstered

271

his gun and half turned to the back door.

The owner made the mistake of moving, reaching toward the table, perhaps for something concealed in the drawer. The masked man's right hand shot forward like the head of a striking snake; a wicked little sleeve gun spatted against his palm, blazed.

The owner fell to the floor screaming, pawing at his bullet-smashed shoulder with reddening fingers, the sleeve of his shirt dyed scarlet. The masked man glanced at him impersonally and walked out.

At the boom of the derringer, the fight in the bar room had abruptly ceased. Yells and curses arose. A bartender rushed to the back room door, found it locked. He seized a table and began battering it open, others joining in with stools and benches. Behind the stubbornly resisting door, the screams of the wounded owner continued.

Finally the splintered door swung

open, hanging by one hinge. The crowd rushed in.

But the two men who had been 'fighting' so vigorously a few minutes before were not of their number. They had unobtrusively drifted through the swinging doors to vanish into the night.

The Javelina was a fair simulacrum of a madhouse on a busy day. The head bartender, somewhat experienced in such matters, managed to do a fairly good job of slackening the blood flow from the wounded shoulder, and the owner gasped out what had happened. Nobody, it seemed, connected the scuffle at the bar with the robbery.

A doctor was sent for, and the *jefe politico*, which was a signal for certain gentlemen to discreetly depart, apparently preferring not to be present when the police chief arrived.

And the irrigation workers, not caring to get mixed up in such an affair south of the Rio Grande, also got the heck out of there.

It was some of the workers who brought a rather highly colored but fairly accurate version of the outrage to La Luz, to which everybody, including Walt Slade and Sheriff Calder, listened with interest.

"Well, our *amigo* was in a *cantina* tonight, but not the one Estevan has been watching," Slade observed dryly.

"So you figure it was Palmer and his two hellions?" the sheriff asked.

"Of course," *El Halcón* replied. "Has all the marks of his handiwork. Had the fake fight staged at the bar to hold everybody's attention while he opened the supposed-to-be-locked back door with a key made from a wax impression, a simple chore for such as he, or, if the key was in the lock inside the room, turned it with a slender pair of long-nosed pliers. Nothing new about it, but handled expertly, as Palmer does everything, it worked."

"Well, anyhow, thank Pete, it didn't happen in our bailiwick," said Calder. "It's a chore for the boys down here. Think we oughta go over there?"

"I suppose so," Slade answered. "Chances are we won't be able to learn anything, but the police chief might have something to tell us; he's a shrewd old geezer.

"We'll be back before long," he told Dolores. "Tell Clark to wait for us."

"Oh, he'll wait, all right," Dolores replied. "Look at them over there at the table — '*At last I've found you!*'"

"You're good at promoting romances," Slade said smilingly.

"Yes, some times," she answered, the blue eyes somber.

When they arrived at the Javelina, they found both the doctor and the police chief already there, the latter busy asking questions and taking notes. He greeted them cheerfully.

"Of this, as my *amigo* Calder would call it, rumhole, I have long been suspicious," he said to Slade. "I believe, though not able to prove, that *hombres* here drinking unwisely have been robbed. Would you not call what happened tonight perhaps the retributive justice, *Capitán?*"

"There's an old saying: 'As ye sow, so shall ye reap.' This could be an instance," Slade replied, recalling his own experience in the place.

"How's the patient?" he asked, glancing at the bandage owner, who was sitting in a chair and not looking happy.

"The *médico* says recover he will," answered the chief. "With him I will later talk. Perhaps the lesson he has learned. You must go? *Buenas noches, Capitán*; return soon. And you, *Señor* Sheriff."

When they reached La Luz, they found the crowd had pretty well thinned out. The girls had retired to the dressing room to change. Clark and Dolores were awaiting them.

"Say!" exclaimed the engineer. "That little girl Miss Dolores introduced me to is all right. As I told her when we said goodnight, I'm coming back."

"That's the spirit," Slade approved. "You need something to take your mind off your work now and then. Be good for you. All set to amble, Dolores?"

21

THE following afternoon, Sheriff Calder remarked, "Well, the hellion made a good haul last night."

"Yes, he did," Slade conceded. "But don't feel complacent; it will only whet his appetite for more. I'd say he's money mad, along with his other nice maniacal tendencies. He'll be on the move again soon."

"I suppose so," growled the sheriff. "And what we are going to do about it I'm hanged if I know."

"Back to the guessing game," Slade replied. "Check all possibilities and try to anticipate what he may have in mind."

"Nice prospect, drat it!" Calder grumbled. "Clark headed back to the camp before you got up. Looked starryeyed. Wouldn't be surprised if he ends up pulling in double harness. Oh, well, may be the best thing for him; never can tell."

"Why didn't you ever try it, Tom?" Slade asked.

The sheriff's gaze wandered about the room, centered on the sun glowing window.

"She died," he said simply.

Slade leaned forward, placed a hand on the old peace officer's knee. His deep voice was all music, his cold eyes all kindness when he spoke. "I'm sorry, Tom. I didn't know, or I wouldn't have spoken in jest."

"I know you wouldn't have, Walt," Calder answered. "It happened thirty years and more ago. That's a long time, but I guess memory don't take 'count of the years. Let's have some coffee."

Estevan appeared, in a bad temper. "The *ladrón* his *cantina* in is," he reported. "The no move he makes. I myself no more keep watch, for me he may suspect. So *amigos* unknown to him keep the watch and to me report."

"That's smart," Slade said. "He's a clever one and may have caught on to the fact that you have been keeping tabs on him."

"So thought I," Estevan agreed.

The next day Estevan was still in a bad temper, and the day that followed. For Palmer made no move and spent most of his time in the *cantina*, appearing to be in a cheerful mood.

This caused *El Halcón* to experience qualms of uneasiness. There was little doubt but that the outlaw leader had something in mind and could be expected to act at any moment.

When the fourth day rolled around with nothing happening, the suspense approached the unbearable, at least to Slade's way of thinking.

"Maybe the hellion is figuring to pull out," suggested Calder.

"If he can manage to make one more big haul, he might do that," Slade replied. "He must know the loop is closing around him and may act accordingly. But I don't think he will without another big haul, and for that I'll wager he is planning all this time, perhaps foreseeing an opportunity to which we are giving no thought."

"Blast it! I reckon you're right," the sheriff said wearily. "Oh, the devil! Let's mosey out and amble around a while. Might clear our minds a bit; mine's as foggy as a December morning."

Slade was agreeable, and they proceeded to act on the suggestion, wandering aimlessly about the town. They paused at the water's edge and gazed at the turgid Rio Grande, for the river was very high, rolling swiftly to merge with the blue waters of the Gulf.

"Looks like with all the rest of our troubles we may be in for a flood," growled Calder. "Must have been raining like heck up around the Devil's River country."

"Yes, appears that way," Slade agreed.

With an angry sunset blazing red in

the west, they returned to the office in a somber mood. They were barely seated comfortably with coffee and smokes when Estevan entered, looking pleased and excited, his black eyes snapping.

"*Capitán*" he said, "the *ladrón* Palmer and *hombres* two ride. Across the bridge they rode. My *amigo* who watched also rode, keeping the well back. They rode the quite openingly, talking and laughing together, not trying their movements to conceal, and, said my *amigo* never did they back look. West they turned on the river trail. My *amigo* thought it not wise to farther follow, so he to me returned. I thought *Capitán* should know."

"Yes," Slade answered. "And they never looked back?"

"So said my *amigo*."

"But what in blazes could they have in mind to the west of here?" the sheriff put in. "The Los Indios stage doesn't pull out until day after tomorrow; the Alice stage, a day later. What *could* the blankety-blanks have in mind?"

Slade sat silent, the concentration furrow deep between his black brows, a sure sign *El Halcón* was doing some hard and fast thinking. He rolled and lighted a cigarette before replying, the others watching him expectantly.

"I think," he said at last, "that for once *Senõr* Palmer slipped just a little by being a trifle too obvious."

"Yes?"

"Yes. He knows very well that somebody has been keeping tabs on him. So he made sure to give the impression that he and his two followers were riding west on some legitimate errand to fool whoever was keeping watch and anybody else who might notice. Courting observation, as it were. In my opinion, he has nothing to the west in mind. After dark, he will circle back to Brownsville and slip into town undetected, with his final big haul nicely planned."

"And that is?"

"The Brownsville bank."

"The bank!" the sheriff repeated

incredulously. "The bank has never been robbed or burgled."

"And so of course it never will be," Slade retorted, mildly sarcastic.

"That big safe would be a hard nut to crack," protested the sheriff.

"No nut is too hard for Palmer to crack, given opportunity and a little time," Slade rejoined.

"And they have a watchman patrolling inside and outside the bank," Calder pointed out.

"And if we don't look after him, they'll have a dead watchman on their hands come daybreak tomorrow," Slade countered grimly. "You know him, of course?"

"Yep, knowed him for years," the sheriff replied. "A nice old jigger."

"So we'll have him with us when we set our trap," Slade said.

"But won't the devils miss him not being around and get suspicious?"

"I think I will be able to take care of that," Slade answered.

"Blast it!" the sheriff growled. "I just

thought about it. I let the deputies go over to Zeke Combes' place to take part in a little birthday party he's throwing. Heck knows when they'll get back, and I reckon it's too late to send for them."

"To do so we would be just a trifle obvious," Slade said. "You, Estevan and myself should be able to handle the situation."

"Of the certainty," said Estevan, caressing the haft of his knife.

"And the old watchman ain't bad company in a pinch," added Calder. "Yep, we'll make out; I'm itchin' for a chance to line sights with the sidewinders."

"Of course all this deduction of mine may be erroneous," Slade said. "But somehow, I figure it's a straight hunch. We won't make any moves until well after dark. Then we'll get busy and see if we can arrange a surprise for 'amigo Palmer."

"If you figure it's a straight hunch, it is," the sheriff declared positively.

"Hope so," Slade replied. "Now I'll be wanting a shirt, a pair of overalls, a hat, a bit of straw, one of the spare guns you have in the drawer and a length of twine. I think Agosto, the stable keeper, will be able to supply everything needed aside from the gun."

"And that's right here ready to hand," said Calder, opening the drawer and peering inside. "Now what?"

"Now, shortly, we'll amble over to the Blue Bell and lay a foundation of chuck to strengthen us," Slade decided.

"That's plumb sensible," Calder nodded. "With a snort or two to hold it down."

They took their time at dinner, and it was two hours past full dark when Slade led the way to the stable and began making preparations. Agosto provided all that was needed. The shirt and the overalls were secured together and stuffed with straw until they were well plumped out. Calder fetched the night watchman, a bright-eyed, elderly individual who appeared excited and not at all displeased with what was in prospect.

The bank building, somewhat isolated from the busier streets, sat in a grove — there were groves everywhere in Brownsville — and it was very dark under the trees where Shadow, the sheriff's cayuse and Estevan's mustang, cinched up, were ensconced. The watchman let the posse in with his key, and they got busy by the dim light of a turned-low bracket lamp.

The 'dummy' was placed in a chair, leaning forward over the table. With the hat on top, it gave a very creditable resemblance to a man drowsing with his head pillowed on his arms.

"By gosh! It looks more human than you do, Pete," Calder said to the watchman, who countered with a few remarks not complimentary to law-enforcement officers, so called, in general and the one present in particular.

"But it will sure look nacherel to any horned toad peekin' through the window," he admitted.

Slade secured the gun to the table leg, the muzzle elevated so that a slug from it would harmlessly strike the wall, high up. To the trigger he carefully fastened one end of the twine. The other he fastened to the knob of the door that opened outward. Then he cocked the gun.

"And anybody trying to open that door from the outside will get the scare of his ornery life," Calder predicted.

They left the building by the barred back door, Slade knowing that Palmer, who was undoubtedly familiar with the layout of the bank, would not try to enter by way of that door. They took up their position under the trees, beside the horses and quite close to the office door, of which they had a clear, though shadowy view.

"Now all we can do is wait and hope for the best," Slade said. "Ought to know pretty soon if my hunch is a straight one. Yes, I think we can risk a smoke; they'll hardly show before midnight, if they show at all, and it lacks nearly an hour of that."

The time dragged past on leaden feet. Midnight came and went, and Slade began to grow doubtful. And then his keen ears caught a sound of approaching hoofbeats that paused at the nearby rack outside the building.

"They're coming," he whispered. "Get set. You do the talking, Tom; have to give them a chance to surrender. They won't; so shoot straight."

Several moments of heightening suspense followed; then abruptly shadowy forms materialized by the bank door. There was a slight clicking sound. The door swung open, slowly.

Boom said the forty-five secured to the table leg. The shadowy forms ducked with startled exclamations.

"Up!" roared the sheriff. "You are under arrest!"

The forms whirled to the direction of his voice. Guns blazed. Lead whined past the unseen posse. Slade drew and shot with both hands. His companion's guns echoed the bellow of the big Colts.

One of the forms fell sprawling. Then a second. But the third, tall, broad-shouldered, ducking, weaving, sped to the hitch rack. There was a clatter of hoofs scudding down Levee Street to the bridge.

Slade bounded to where Shadow stood, hurled himself into the saddle.

"Trail, feller, trail!" he shouted. The great black leaped forward, going at top speed, slowly overhauling Palmer's tall bay. Soon Slade was within shooting distance, but he held his fire, there being people on the street who might stop a flying slug. Also, he must give Palmer his chance to surrender.

Slade had a very good notion of what the cunning and foresighted outlaw leader had in mind. Could he get across to Mexico, where *El Halcón* had no positive jurisdiction, even though he was not able to distance his pursuer, he could surrender himself to the state authorities and in all likelihood ultimately escape.

They boomed up the approach to where the span leveled off. A few more strides and the fugitive would be well in Mexico.

"Palmer, pull up or I'll kill you!" Slade thundered. "Pull up, I say!"

Palmer's answer was to whirl his mount almost in full stride. His gun spurted fire. The slug fanned Slade's face. Another came even closer. He flung his Colts to the front, squeezed both triggers.

Palmer screamed, a scream that crescendoed to a horrible, blood-bubbling shriek. He rose in his stirrups, pitched sideways from the saddle and onto the bridge rail. For a moment he toppled, then plunged over the rail to rush down, arms and legs thrashing widly, to the black water of the Rio Grande. He struck the surface with a mighty splash and vanished from view. He did not reappear.

Pulling to a halt, Slade gazed down at the hurrying river, its dark expanse dimpled with stars. Rolling a cigarette, he waited for Calder and Estevan to appear, which they did a few minutes later.

"Did you get him?" the sheriff asked.

"I venture to believe so," Slade replied. "He went into the river, and even were his wound not mortal — and I think it was — a badly injured man would never be able to breast that flood-current and reach the shore. Yes, we can rest assured it's trail's end for Eldon Palmer. Anybody hurt?"

"Pete, the watchman, was cutting loose a string of cuss words, so I reckon he got nicked, but not seriously." Calder answered. "Guess we'd better go see."

When they reached the bank, they found quite a crowd gathered, listening eagerly to old Pete's vivid account of the affair. He mopped a slightly bullet-gashed cheek, of which he was evidently very proud.

Nobody had touched the two bodies.

Beside them was a sack containing a hand drill and bits, mute evidence of what their intentions had been.

Clint, the bank president, put in an appearance to say a number of commendatory things to the posse, Slade in particular.

"Yes, you saved us plenty," he said. "Shut up, Pete; you'll get a raise in wages for the part you played."

The bodies were packed to the sheriff's office and laid out on the floor.

"Guess they make it a clean sweep," Calder observed. "Yep, chore finished. Reckon you'll be moving on, eh, Walt?"

"Not for a few days," Slade replied. "I want to visit with Lanham and his wife, drop in on old Zeke Combs and have a last gabfest with Amado and Taylor Ross. Keep your blade thirsty till I get back, Estevan."

Four days later, Dolores, his until-we-meet-again kiss warm on her lips, watched him ride away, tall and graceful atop his great black horse, to where duty called and new adventure waited.

THE END

FIGHTING RAMROD
Charles N. Heckelmann

Most men would have cut their losses, but Frazer counted the bullets in his guns and said he'd soak the range in blood before he'd give up another inch of what was his.

LONE GUN
Eric Allen

Smoke Blackbird had been away too long. The Lequires had seized the Blackbird farm, forcing the Indians and settlers off, and no one seemed willing to fight! He had to fight alone.

THE THIRD RIDER
Barry Cord

Mel Rawlins wasn't going to let anything stand in his way. His father was murdered, his two brothers gone. Now Mel rode for vengeance.

ARIZONA DRIFTERS
W. C. Tuttle

When drifting Dutton and Lonnie Steelman decide to become partners they find that they have a common enemy in the formidable Thurston brothers.

TOMBSTONE
Matt Braun

Wells Fargo paid Luke Starbuck to outgun the silver-thieving stagecoach gang at Tombstone. Before long Luke can see the only thing bearing fruit in this eldorado will be the gallows tree.

HIGH BORDER RIDERS
Lee Floren

Buckshot McKee and Tortilla Joe cut the trail of a border tough who was running Mexican beef into Texas. They stopped the smuggler in his tracks.

BRETT RANDALL, GAMBLER
E. B. Mann

Larry Day had the choice of running away from the law or of assuming a dead man's place. No matter what he decided he was bound to end up dead.

THE GUNSHARP
William R. Cox

The Eggerleys weren't very smart. They trained their sights on Will Carney and Arizona's biggest blood bath began.

THE DEPUTY OF SAN RIANO
Lawrence A. Keating and
Al. P. Nelson

When a man fell dead from his horse, Ed Grant was spotted riding away from the scene. The deputy sheriff rode out after him and came up against everything from gunfire to dynamite.